Parents from Space

PARENTS FROM SPACE

by George Bowering

Cover illustration by Janice Poltrick Donato

ROUSSAN
PUBLISHERS INC.

Roussan Publishers Inc. acknowledges with appreciation the assistance of the Canada Council in the production of this book.

Copyright © 1994 by George Bowering

Legal deposit 3rd quarter 1994
National Library of Canada
Quebec National Library
ISBN 1-896184-00-6

Canadian Cataloging in Publication Data

Bowering, George, 1935-
Parents from space

(Out of this world series)
ISBN 1-896184-00-6

I. Title. II. Series

PS8503.0875P3 1994   jC813'.54   C94-900565-7
PZ7.B69Pa 1994

Printed and bound in Canada

for Gumpy

Here I am, an utter stranger, getting ready to tell you about something you're probably not going to believe. I had it all planned out to introduce myself and my family and my three best friends and how we like to review films, but the people that turn stories into books told me to forget all that stuff. Start right in with the strange stuff from outer space, they said. What if I explain exactly how I got to be a film critic, I suggested. Outer space, they said. What can I do? You're on your own.

Anyway, here it was Monday morning under a blue sky, and I was riding a bus downtown. I had a few dollars I had made from selling an old pipe rack I found in the attic. I was on my way to the Downtown Twelve to see a film about the difficulties of communication for human beings in urban America. It was called *Spilled Intestines* VI. I think the Roman numerals were there to make reference to the gladiatorial nature of the action in the film.

Looking out the window of the bus, I saw a kid about my age come running out the front door of a bungalow on Bristle Street. I could see from where I was sitting that his eyes were open wide, showing a lot of white. He was running with his hands held at arm's length in front of him, just like the characters in certain inferior comic strips. Behind him came two adults, probably his father and mother, waving their hands at him and shouting. And behind them came two more adults waving their hands, and then two more adults waving their hands. That was unusual enough, but there was something even more unusual.

All three sets of parents looked exactly like each other.

That poor kid, I thought, as the bus chugged away, shaking up my entire innards, I would go screaming and running out of my house too if I had that many relatives shouting at me.

I saw most of *Spilled Intestines* VI and went to the nearby Food Fair to sit and write the first draft of my review. I always went to the Food Fair if I was reviewing a downtown movie. The Food Fair is in the basement under Rain Street, between two big department store shopping arcades. In the Food Fair you can get really bad fast food from thirty different countries. Usually I get a couple of tacos and something called "Mexi-Spuds" and pour brown hot sauce all over them and wash them down with some skim milk while I sit at a round table and write out my review.

I was being a little hard on *Spilled Intestines* VI, lightening my scorn by pretending to be indulgent, if you know what I mean. I was at a disadvantage, because I had not seen *Spilled Intestines* III and IV and V.

Here is a part of what I was writing in pencil in one of

those little secretarial ring binders: "Director Irving Slatz might have considered the tastes of his more northerly audience, and taken advantage of the natural excitement of blood spilled on fresh snow. Instead we get the usual images of scattered brains and organs against Los Angeles walls...."

I was so intent on my sentences that I did not notice the figure who filled the plastic chair across the round table from me. My unconscious might have noticed that the figure was not carrying a food tray.

"Hi, Neville. Are you killing with kindness?"

I looked up, and there was Vivienne. I immediately dropped my sentence and the pencil I was making it with. Viv was sitting very still and quiet. This was not the Viv that one usually saw. She is the kind of person who can not come into a room, even a huge room like the Food Fair, without having everyone looking at her. She even walks with a kind of extravagance. She walks the way Marge Champion dances, as if there were a rumour that we were running out of floors.

But she was definitely not her usual self right now. I looked at her gently, something not usually needed.

"What's cookin', good lookin'?"

I thought that would relax her.

"Neville!"

She was not relaxed.

"What is it, Viv?"

"My parents," she whispered. It was perhaps the first time I had ever heard Viv whisper.

"So what else is new?" I asked.

"Listen, Neville."

"Okay."

"When I came downstairs this morning the first thing I saw was my mother. She asked me why I hadn't brushed my hair. Then my father came into the kitchen. He told me I had bad breath. Then my mother came into the kitchen. She said my socks didn't match. Then my father came into the kitchen—"

"Wait a minute," I said. "They were already in the kitchen, if I've got the story right."

"You've got the story right. But they kept coming into the kitchen. After the third mother and third father, I beat it."

"Couldn't stand all the criticism, I suppose."

"Neville! This is serious."

"I know. I'm sorry. Look, it seems as if you have been under some kind of strain. Too many Judy Garland movies, maybe. Maybe you were still dreaming and only *thought* you had come downstairs. That happens to me a lot."

Viv looked at me as if I were something she saw when she picked up a rock. I was ready to apologize for anything.

Then Harry showed up. He knew my Monday morning habits. He plunked himself down at the round table. He was wearing a Tacoma Tigers baseball cap backward on his head.

"I've got two sets of parents," he said, his eyes looking at the thing that was not there.

"I've got three," said Viv.

"Mine look like identical twins," said Harry.

"Triplets here," said Viv.

"I've got to have a Diet Creme Soda," said Harry.

I got drinks for all three of us. Now I didn't have bus fare home, but I had hopes and friends. When I sat down again, Viv was holding Harry's hand. Now I had no doubt. This was really serious.

"What did your parents say to you?" asked Viv.

"One said I had to wash the car. The second said I had to mow the lawn. The third said I had to clean the outside windows, and the fourth was just saying something about the loose boards in the fence when I hit the trail," said Harry.

He pulled the straw out of his Creme Soda and gulped it straight out of the can.

"I know what it is," he said.

"What *what* is?" we both asked him.

"I'm not going to say anything else till we talk to Feet," he said.

There were two cars in the driveway of Feet's place on Fogswept Boulevard, an old yellowish-brown Volkswagen bus with flower decals all over it, and a brand new black

Mercedes sedan. There was a shiny white cabin cruiser on a trailer in the carport on the side of the house. The front of the house was covered with ivy, and there was hardly any grass in front of the place, just piles and heaps of bushes and trees that looked as if they came from somewhere in the Orient. The front door knocker was in the shape of the old hippy peace sign, but it was made of solid brass.

It seemed pretty quiet. We didn't know whether to go up and knock or hang around, hoping to see something of Feet. It was a quiet neighbourhood. We had been there five minutes and no cars had come by, just one middle-aged woman jogging in a pink track suit and a middle-aged man on a bicycle. We couldn't even *hear* any traffic.

Then I saw movement at an upstairs window. There was a face beside the curtain for a moment. I looked harder and saw that there were faces at several windows. I nudged Viv and she nudged Harry. The faces were not all that clear but they looked a lot alike.

"Psssst!"

I looked at Viv and Harry. They looked at each other and at me.

"Psssssssssst!"

We all looked where we were supposed to look, at the jacaranda tree or whatever it was what separated Feet's yard from the huge yard next door. There she was, poking her head around the trunk of the tree, gesturing toward the street. We looked at each other again and headed for the street. When we got to the corner, there was Feet, waiting for us.

"They...they..."

"How many have you got?" asked Harry.

"Three. Four! Four sets," she managed to say.

"Mine nagged at me till I had to get out of the house," said Viv.

"Mine kept thinking of chores for me to do," said Harry.

"Sometimes I think I would like to trade you both," said Feet, somewhat settled down.

"What do you mean?" I asked, because I didn't have a parents story of my own to tell. Not a new one, anyway.

"Oh, they are so *good*," said Feet. "They do everything *right*. Only they call it *correct*. Make sure you have your oat bran, Dear. Remember your blood sugar count, Honey. Now it is three times worse. I don't believe that shirt is made of natural fibres, Darling. I wouldn't wear that kind of lipstick, Precious. That company engages in incorrect activities concerning the wilderness."

"Boy, oh, boy, I see what you mean," I said.

"I don't even *wear* lipstick."

"Aha!" said Harry.

"Aha what?" asked Viv, her nose nearly touching Harry's nose.

Harry looked as if he had decided something he didn't want to decide. He turned his cap around so that the Tiger was at the front. We all looked at him and maintained our quiet. I felt as if we were in an early Eric Rohmer film.

"I never thought they would be able to change their appearance too," said Harry, as if he were talking to himself.

13

"Harry, what are you talking about?"

"I've got to have a Hawaiian Punch," said Harry. "Get me a Hawaiian Punch, and I will tell you all I know about what's going on."

Harry would not say a word about the multiplying parents all the way to the Blam Cafe on Kaiser Street. The Blam Cafe isn't a cafe, really. It is just a counter in a wall and a bunch of benches along long tables, where people read the crumbly old newspapers lying around there, and drink cans of pop and eat triangular sandwiches that come wrapped in clear plastic you can't get off without wrecking the sandwiches.

We never eat the sandwiches there. Usually the only kinds they have are chopped egg salad on brown and cheese slices on white. Both kinds of sandwiches taste like porcelain, even after you get them put all together again. Each of us had tried both sandwiches once.

Now we had four cans of stuff. Harry had Hawaiian Punch. Viv had Iced Tea. Feet had Reel Froot. And I had Diet Grape Soda.

Harry had his Tacoma Tigers cap on sideways, the peak above his right ear. He did not look at us, but stared out the window of the Blam Cafe. There were posters for old rock and roll concerts on most of the windows. You could look out between them and catch a glimpse of people going by. At this time of day on Kaiser Street those people were mainly single mothers pushing strollers and looking for a bargain on disposable diapers.

"Harry," said Feet, "I can't wait all afternoon. I can't wait while you go through all your rituals and routines. Tell us what you know about our parents."

"They are not your parents," he said, his voice quiet and monotonous. "Not all of them."

"That's pretty obvious, Harry," said Viv. "The last time I counted I had one father and one mother, and I thought that was one too many at times."

Out of the corner of my eye I saw a blur going by the window. I popped to the door and looked out. I saw a teenage boy carrying his skate board and running down the sidewalk toward the beach. When I came back to the bench my friends asked me what I had seen. I told them it was a kid running for his life. They were not surprised.

"Harry, explain," suggested Viv.

"Well," said Harry, "it all has to do with those voices I heard on the satellite receiver. The way I have pieced the story together goes like this. These extra parents are from outer space."

"Harry, too many early morning movies," suggested Viv.

"Okay, you explain it," he said.

"Go on, my friend," I said in what I hoped was a calming voice.

"These extra parents are from outer space. They came to Earth or at least our part of it, and somehow managed to make themselves look like Earthlings and talk our language."

"We Earthlings have 620 languages," said Feet. "Do you think they know them all?"

"If they can come across the universe and find a way of landing in the Pacific Northwest, they can learn our languages, even English," I said. "What I would like to know is: how do they manage to change from their regular shape to our shape?"

Harry put his cap on frontward. He raised a hand and pointed his forefinger into the air above his head.

"Maybe they don't have a regular shape," he said.

"Everything has a shape," said Viv.

"Not necessarily a physical shape. Memories about your first taste of asparagus with cheese sauce, for instance, have shape, but no visible shape."

"What do you mean? Are these people...."

"People?"

"Creatures."

"Yes, these creatures may live and travel primarily as something that doesn't have physical shape."

"Like memories? Memories travelling through space, I don't think so, Harry," said Viv.

"Not necessarily memories," said Harry. "That was just an example of something that doesn't have physical shape but still has some kind of shape. What about something like clear sharp ideas? Maybe on their planet or wherever they live, the main life form is ideas. Maybe they don't have to travel on space ships."

"Maybe they just *think* they are zooming across the universe?"

"Well, maybe for them thinking *is* zooming."

"Ideas, Harry?" Viv was not a very convincing skeptic.

"I could be wrong," said Harry. "As a scientist I have to say that I probably am."

"Harry, I don't want this to be true," said Feet.

"Science must, however, keep itself free of sentiment," said Harry.

"Science doesn't have to go home tonight," said Feet.

I got up and threw my empty can into the recycling barrel, and the others followed my example. No one missed the barrel. I took that for a good sign. We walked into the bright sunshine of Kaiser Street. It was five in the afternoon. We saw the people who had to change out of suits and dresses heading for the beach with rolled-up towels under their arms.

Apparently the parent invasion had not reached the newsrooms yet.

We went to the beach and sat on the sea wall, where we could watch the Portuguese families putting out their smelt nets in the shallow water. We had to figure out what to do.

"Neville?"

"Yes, Feet."

"You are the only one who hasn't seen extra parents yet. I think we should go to your place and check it out before we do anything else. If we run into multi-parents there, we can think about going to the radio stations."

So that is what we decided to do. The last thing I saw before we left the beach was a shiny little fish with its head caught in one of the nets. It was thrashing its body in the sunlight, a strong little creature from under the sea.

I don't think it meant anything, just a little piece of success for one of the Portuguese families.

When we arrived at my place we arrived like a small squad of guerrilla jungle people, like freedom fighters in a dictator's yard. We burst in the door and fanned out, our backs to the walls, attack rifles at the ready. Well, we didn't have any attack rifles, but we felt as if maybe we should have. Or maybe we had seen too many advertisements for recent American run-and-gun movies. I don't think any of us had actually seen any of the movies, but we had certainly seen the ads.

"I feel like Chuck Schwartzeneggar," whispered Harry.

"That's *Arnold*, Harry. His name is Arnold," Viv said.

"Check the upstairs," I ordered. "Feet, you get the kitchen and back yard. Viv, take the basement. I'll cover you and check out the downstairs bathroom."

We moved like the U.S. Marine Corpses in all the recent Vietnam movies, a few feet at a time, leaping from cover to cover. I jumped into the bathroom, my imaginary assault rifle held in front of me. There was no one in the bathroom. I slid the shower door open. In the shower there was nothing but my sister's blouse on a coat hanger, hanging off the shower head.

"Neville!"

That was Feet's voice.

"Back yard, everyone!" I ordered.

My parents were sitting in their lawn chairs, holding pieces of the late edition *Moon*. My father is the main headline writer for the *Moon*, but today was the first day of his annual vacation. In fact he was holding his last pre-vacation piece of work. STRIPPER BARES ALL TO JUDGE, it said. My parents were silent. We had them surrounded.

"Hi, Mr and Mrs Neatby," said Viv. She was the perfect one for breaking the ice on all social occasions.

"Yeah, hi, Mom and Dad," I added.

"What is all this running around and shouting all about?" asked my mother.

"Mom, are you and Dad alone?"

"Well, we *were* until you lot came crashing in."

"No relatives dropped in all at once?"

"Not that I am aware of," said my mother. "Your shoe laces are untied," she added. She has told me that at least once every day since my ninth birthday.

I looked at my friends. They would normally be sprawling on the lawn by now, but there was a certain vigilance still, as if more parents might come over the fence at any moment.

"There's no one who looks like you and Dad around? No one gone to the store or anything?"

"There's no one in the world that looks like your mother," said my father. It is an opportunity like this that brings him out of his habitual silence.

"Isn't that nice?" said Viv.

"Don't bet on it, Dad," I said.

"What is all this noise about?" asked my mother, angrily scratching a faulty match against the match folder. I waited till she had got her cigarette lit and swallowed the first cloud of smoke.

"There's something funny going on around here," I said.

"What else is new?" asked my mother, glancing at my father.

"There are too many parents," said Harry.

"You'll miss us when we're gone," said my father. I liked that one.

"What Harry means is that there is an invasion of extra parents. There are at least four sets of them at my place, all identical," said Feet.

My mother has more patience and respect for Feet than for my other friends. This is probably because she has seen her address.

"Is this an invasion from outer space, by any chance?" she asked, handling her cigarette the way Joan Crawford used to handle hers. All the mothers and grandmothers that still smoke have studied Joan Crawford.

"It's serious, Mrs Neatby," said Viv. "I have three sets at my place, all identical."

"I presume you mean that the males resemble one

another and that the females resemble one another," said my father, the newspaper still open between his hands. He had that way of handling the paper that all newspaper guys have. You can tell a newspaper guy from the way he folds and holds a newspaper.

"I think you lot might think about taking a rest from the movies," suggested my mother.

I started walking toward the kitchen door.

"Let's go, you lot," I said.

Viv sat down.

"Let's go, you guys," I said, and stared at her. Then I walked away. Harry and Feet caught up to me. Viv got up and made sure she walked slowly in our direction. Viv very rarely walked slowly.

They followed me into the house, helped me grab a certain amount of food from the fridge, and followed me out the front door and down the street. We kept walking until we came to Kaiser Park. Then we kept walking till we came to a part that did not have any dog turds on the grass or idiots with portable radios in the neighbourhood.

Then we sat down and started in on our picnic. We ate just about everything we had brought, though a planned meal might have been more enjoyable and even more wholesome. Cheese crackers with mayonnaise might be all right. Dry Barley Blimps are edible, I suppose. Onion pickles are a personal favourite of mine. Viv was happy about the Mexi-Spuds. But no one wanted to eat the cauliflower, not even with a mayonnaise dip.

We looked around the park. There were the usual parents with babies, parents with toddlers, parents with kids and dogs. We did not notice any duplicates. Maybe parents from outer space did not go to parks. Maybe they were lurking in the kitchens of these unsuspecting moms and dads.

"So what does this mean?" I asked. I often asked that question, especially when it looked as if I had to bring one of our regular Sunday evening film review club meetings to order. I didn't mind so much as long as *they* didn't mind.

"What does *what* mean, Neville?" That was Feet, of course. She could assume her preferred tone of voice with an entire cheese cracker in her mouth.

A dog with matted black hair came by and requested a snack. Harry held out a handful of Barley Blimps. The dog sniffed them a moment, then turned and trotted away, in search of lunch across the fields. Harry tossed the Barley Blimps into his own mouth.

"Well, among us all I am the only one who has just one set of parents," I said.

"Or so it seems," said Harry. At least I *think* that's what he said around his mouthful of Barley Blimps.

"Or so it seems," I agreed. "Either there is something about me that makes me immune to parental parthenogenesis, or–"

"Or this is just a fluke," said Feet. "Maybe one kid out of four gets to keep his regular quota of parents."

"Or grandparents," I said. "I just thought–where is my granny? Did anyone see her in the house? Maybe when the parents arrive the grandparents all disappear. You three should phone your grandparents and see whether they are still around. Maybe the grandparents are all in rocket ships, being transported to the Planet of the Old Folks. Maybe–"

Viv jumped up and clamped her hand over my mouth.

"Mmmppnfg ghmmph," I said, waving my arms.

Harry held my arms.

"I saw your grandmother at your place," said Viv, her face right in front of my face. She spoke slowly and clearly. It is not often that you get to hear Viv speaking slowly.

"Hmmgh," I said.

"She was sitting in the wingback chair in her room, knitting something," said Viv.

I pulled her hand off my mouth.

"She makes me an Indian sweater with the design of two horses on it every year around this time," I said. "I have suggested that I don't need another sweater. I have suggested that I wouldn't mind just a traditional Indian design. I have bought other patterns and put them in her room. Doesn't matter. I get horses."

"I've never seen you in a sweater with horses," said Harry.

"Do you want one?"

"Sure," said Harry. Harry will wear things that other people won't wear. I have always known this.

"Oh no," I said.

Viv had her hand ready again.

"I just thought of another possibility," I said.

"Speak," said Feet.

"What if those people we saw in my back yard aren't my parents. What if they came from outer space and did something with my parents."

"Maybe that isn't your granny in the wingback chair," suggested Harry.

"Yeah," said Feet. "Look on the sunny side. If she is a granny from outer space, maybe she will knit something besides horses."

"Get serious," I said.

"About grannies from space?" asked Feet.

"About all those extra parents in your house. Where are you going to sleep tonight?"

They all looked at me. How was I going to explain this to my parents? If they *were* my parents.

On the way to my place we had to pass the Otligger house. It's a great big castle kind of place, with a bunch of pillars holding up a little roof in front of the front door, where you can drive up in your car and park and stay dry or shady or whatever you want. Jamie Otligger was an only child, a rich kid about eleven years old. He goes to a private school where they play cricket and wear ties with stripes on them. Before this day I don't think we ever said a word to each other.

Across the street from the Otligger house we saw Jamie Otligger sitting on the sidewalk, with his feet in the gutter and his chin in his hands. Beside him was a brand new mountain bike that looked as if it would cost about as much as the normal family car. Jamie Otligger was crying.

We normally wouldn't have paid attention to Jamie Otligger, no matter what he was doing. For one thing, he was just enough younger than us to put him in another world, so to speak. For another thing, he was a lot richer than Harry and Viv and me, and Feet did not want any other rich kid to know that her parents carried briefcases with brass locks on them.

But the poor kid was crying, after all, and we were kind of interested in kids' problems these days.

"Hey, nice bike, Jamie," I said.

He didn't look up at me. He just pointed across the street. There were three more brand new mountain bikes lying on the huge lawn at his place.

"What's the deal, Jamie?" asked Viv.

"They keep giving me stuff," he said. Up till the word "giving" he was crying, but by the end of his sentence he was just talking angrily.

"Let me guess," said Viv. "You have four sets of parents."

"Four fathers and five mothers," he said. "There were five fathers, but one of them disappeared."

"We know how you feel," said Feet.

"You have no idea," said Jamie.

"We are trying to be friendly, despite everything," said Harry, with an ominous edge to his voice. Or at least it was meant to sound ominous.

Jamie pushed up the sleeve of his white shirt. There were four watches on his wrist and lower arm. I looked closely at the names on them. One said Cartier. One said Rolex. One said St. Moritz. One said Movado. They all looked kind of old-fashioned to me, and they all had hands pointing at numbers. I looked at Feet, and I could tell from the look on her face that these four watches would cost enough to feed Harry Fieldstone till he was middle-aged.

Jamie had one watch on his other arm.

"What about that one?" I asked.

"My real mother gave me that one," he said.

"Hmmm," said Viv, who was in her thinking pose, one elbow in the palm of her other hand, one hand under her chin.

"Yes?" asked Harry.

"Hmm," said Viv. "You should know, Jamie, that your parents are just trying to show their love for you, you being an only child and all."

"Just my luck," said Jamie. He was sounding angrier all the time.

"Yeah, you are a really unlucky kid," said Harry, and walked away a little.

"In the last two days they have given me four skateboards, five credit cards, four computers, all different kinds, five CD players—"

"Did you get a satellite dish?" shouted Harry from up the sidewalk.

"I don't watch television," said Jamie. "Never."

"Do you go to movies?" asked Feet.

"No, I read books."

"Did these parents give you any books?" I asked.

"Zero. They gave me four pairs of hightop basketball shoes and five leather jackets."

"Do you have any theories about where all these parents came from?" I asked.

"For a while I was hoping they were a bad dream," said Jamie.

"What are you going to do?" asked Feet.

"I have been thinking about running away from home," said Jamie.

"You could skateboard away from home," shouted Harry.

About ten years ago my mother got all excited about the family going camping, so she ordered lots of the best camping equipment she saw in a Sierra Club catalogue. Tents, Coleman stoves, sleeping bags, canvas washstands, the works. When my mother buys stuff she always makes sure she gets it all and then some. Most people going camping would never bother thinking of shower clogs, for example. We had four pairs of camping shower clogs.

Then we never got around to going camping. So the camping stuff got piled in the garage, along with the scuba diving stuff and the touring bikes. There is no room in the garage for a car. My mother keeps her car under a tree that drips gooey stuff on it, and my father doesn't have a car. He takes a couple of buses to the Vancouver *Moon*.

So that night there were kids in sleeping bags all over our house. Not really all over. My sister would not let any of my friends share her room. I had Harry sleeping on the floor in my room, Viv got the floor in the living room, and Feet got the couch.

Viv told me that my granny came out in the middle of the night to go to the bathroom, and stepped on the bottom end of her sleeping bag.

"Oh," said my granny. "Where in the world did *you* come from?"

"At least it was in the world," answered Viv.

I would never have been able to think that fast in the middle of the night. I think Viv has a second set of nerves or something. I think she is a medical prodigy. I'm glad she's my friend and not my enemy.

"Were there any other suspicious events during the night?" I asked.

"What makes you call your granny's call to nature a suspicious event?"

"Nothing. Nothing. Maybe I'm just nervous. How would *you* like to be the person with just one set of parents?"

"Is that an offer?" asked Viv.

It was very early in the morning, so we were whispering in the kitchen, or at least *I* was. Harry was looking in the fridge. Feet arrived, yawning, her long thick brown hair falling in a tangle over one shoulder. There was light in the sky. Chickadees were zipping to the bird feeder for sunflower seeds and zipping away again. No one else in my family was up yet.

Harry had found the milk. Now he was pouring it over a huge mound of Barley Blimps.

"Neville, show me where your sister's room is," said Feet.

"Okay, but why?"

"I think we should get her in on our problem."

My sister was not pleased at being wakened so early by a person who would tolerate her brother. But she did come to the kitchen without any really loud yelling. Not saying good morning to anyone, she went to the fridge and got out the orange juice carton and drank from it without the aid of a glass.

"Have you noticed anything strange about Mom and Dad?" I asked her.

"Yeah, they made you," she said, and put the orange juice to her mouth again.

"This is serious, Roseanne," said Feet. "Of the four of us, Neville is the only one who has just one set of parents this morning. So far."

My sister made a sardonic grin.

"Thank you for the information. Now if you don't mind, I will go back to my warm bed."

I was in favour of letting her. But eventually the other three managed to get her attention, and to persuade her that we weren't pulling a stunt of some kind.

"So what do you want me to do about it?" she asked.

"Have a check around with your friends, if they're not all in jail," I said.

Viv hit me on the top of my head with the flat of her hand. Get someone to try it on you some time.

"Do check around, if you will, Roseanne. We have to know how widespread this invasion thing is," said Feet.

"How come it isn't in the paper or on TV?" asked my sister.

"That's another thing we have to check on," said Harry, his mouth not entirely empty of Barley Blimps and milk. "It could be there hasn't been time yet. It could be that this is just a little invasion and a few of us happen to be the invaded, which is not likely. It could be there is a conspiracy of silence. That's what happened in this Clark Milland movie I saw a couple weeks ago. You see—"

"All right, Harry," said Feet. "Right now we have to get an idea of how far this thing has spread. Maybe Neville can wheedle something out of his father, about how things are down at the paper."

"He's just gone on vacation," I said.

"Where's he going?"

"Right here," I said. "Here and the magazine store."

As we were headed out the door we saw my mother in her housecoat, carrying an ashtray in one hand and a cigarette in the other. This was half of her normal breakfast, and she was headed to the kitchen for the other half, which would be four cups of coffee.

"We cleaned up and put everything back in the refrigerator," I said cheerily.

"I'll refrigerator you," she said.

We were tripping along Bicuspid Avenue under the chestnut trees as if we knew where we were going and what we were going to do when we got there. Harry was wearing a girl guide camp hat I recognized as having belonged in the olden days to my sister. I didn't upbraid him. He looked kind of stupid, but I guessed he knew that. My sister would have to figure out what to do with the hat he left behind for her.

But we're used to him. I should say that although Harry did not like to brush his teeth all that often, they are not particularly bad, and his breath is okay as boys' breath goes. I should also point out that none of us knew which actor he was referring to—Clark Gable or Ray Milland. Maybe he meant both of them.

Now we slowed down as if we had meant to when we got to the first picnic table in Kaiser Park. There was an old pair of rain-soaked suspenders on it. We left them there while we talked.

"Okay, it is now morning of the next day," said Feet.

"You are pretty sharp," said Harry.

"What I mean, if the groundlings will remain silent for a while, is that we should be able to look at our problem calmly now."

"I'm very calm," said Viv, which was a rare condition for her. I think her scalp follicles were probably gyrating or something.

"What exactly is our problem?" I asked.

"Parents. Parents from Space," said Feet.

"Parents from the Dark Planet," said Harry.

"The revenge of the Alien Parents," said Viv.

"Rough rough," said a dark brown pit bull terrier which came by and showed us his teeth. Harry threw the soggy suspenders as far as he could, and the pit bull muscle-jumped after them and was last seen shaking them hard against his own rear as he disappeared through a hedge full of spider webs.

"I hope *he* doesn't have a bunch of new parents," said Feet.

Viv's eyes opened as wide as saucers.

"I would like to call this meeting to order," I suggested.

"Second that motion," said Harry.

"You don't second a motion to call a meeting to order," said Viv, scorn hurled at poor Harry. Harry pulled the slight floppy brim of his new hat over his eyes.

"I second that correction," said Feet, helpfully.

"Let me begin again," I said. "Shut up and sit down."

"We are all sitting down," said Harry, "except you."

I sat down.

They all looked at me. I guess I was Mister Chairman.

"I don't believe this," I said.

"What?"

"What?"

"Pardon?"

"I mean about the parents. Did we dream it?"

"No," said Viv. "I have never had a bad dream in my life. I come from a family in which such things are discouraged."

"How can you eat peanut butter and tomato sandwiches and not have bad dreams?" enquired Harry.

"Can we stick to the topic on the agenda?" I entreated.

"I stand corrected," said Harry.

"Sit down and shut up," said Viv.

"I have an idea," I said.

"Give," said Viv.

"Maybe this is a movie. Maybe we are the people in a movie." No one said anything. I felt as if I had better not let the silence take over and swallow us up. "An invasion from outer space movie," I specified.

"You are an idiot, Neville," said Feet. She took off one of her sandals and dumped some sand from it onto my knee.

"Is that why they're called sandals?" asked Harry.

"What?"

"Sand, sandals. I mean if you dumped mud out of them would they be called muddles?"

"Can we stick to the subject?" I pleaded.

"Oh sure, monster movies," said Viv.

"Well, look," I said. "Our only experience of such a thing has been in dumb movies, right? So logically, when and if we see this sort of thing happening, we must assume that it is in a movie rather than real life."

"And if Harry falls in love with me, it must be a love movie?" suggested Feet, allowing a probably feigned shiver to cross her shoulders.

"Now *that* would be a monster movie," said Harry.

"I think we are in a movie," I said. "Or at least we should entertain, pardon the pun, that idea till a better one comes along."

"Oh yeah?" shouted Viv.

"Shhhh."

"Oh yeah?" asked Viv in a normal voice. "Look around. Where are all the cameras, and directors sitting in chairs with their names on them, and key grips, and best boys?"

"What the heck are key grips?" asked Harry. "I always meant to ask."

"It doesn't matter," I said. "I didn't say we were actors in a movie. I said we were *in* a movie."

"Like characters?" asked Viv.

"Yeah. I sort of feel like I'm the central character, and you are the supporting characters and we have ninety minutes to get through this story."

"I'm a supporting character?" asked Feet.

"Be that as it may," said Viv.

"We are made up?" asked Harry.

"Or a book," I said.

"What?"

"What?"

"Pardon?"

"A novel," I said.

Silence fell over the picnic table. We could hear traffic at the edges of the park. Harry pulled his hat as best he could low over his eyes. Then he took furtive glances in all directions, including up. Feet dumped her other sandal on my other knee. I could have ducked.

"That's silly," shouted Viv.

"Shhh."

"That's ridiculous," Viv whispered loudly. "I don't know about you, Neville, but I am a completely independent person. Look, I am going to raise my hand."

"Look, she's raising her hand," said Feet.

"I can do anything my brain decides."

"She said."

"What?"

"I said she said. That's what it says in a novel in circumstances such as this. Well, not exactly like this."

"What are you talking about?"

"She asked."

"Neville, I am going to punch you in the forehead with my middle knuckle."

"She threatened. Neville leaned away from her."

I leaned away from her.

Harry had a worried look on his face. He stood up and began walking across the park. He looked as if he would not alter his course for dog turds or wet spots. We all got up and followed him. We were halfway across the park before anyone said anything.

"Who do you think is writing us?" asked Feet.

"Shh."

We walked in silence across the sun-dappled park, in a ragged and aimless group that kept changing shape. Some of us made meaningless gestures from time to time. Our faces were blank, either thoughtful or emptied of thought. We must have looked like a French movie of the Sixties.

Just before the park disappears and the sand of Kannegeiser Beach starts there is an old fashioned park bench, with a curvy bottom and back, painted dark green. On the bench we saw Mr Dropo. Mr Dropo is the father of Willy Dropo, a kid in my Applied Anxiety class last winter.

We approached him. We were not really interested in talking with Mr Dropo, but here he was, sitting on a park bench by the path we had to take to get to the beach and especially to the great french fries and vinegar at the beach concession stand.

"Hello, Mr Dropo," I said.

"Ghhnnn…"

"He replied," said Harry.

Viv held her fist ten centimeters in front of his eyes.

"When you do that," said Harry, "I wish I had a half a grapefruit, like Robert Cagney in *Guys with Dirty Faces.* "

"Grhhnnng…," said Mr Dropo.

He was sitting with his elbows on his knees and his eyes pressed against the palms of his hands. He was wearing his usual outfit, a pair of polyester slacks with a permanently pressed crease and a self-belt, a polo shirt with the picture of a sailboat on the pocket, and white loafers with white ankle socks. That was Mr Dropo. He was the quality control officer at Barney's Meats, the packing house in the east end next to the old train station. Kids always said you should keep your dog out of Mr Dropo's yard.

"Mr Dropo, what's wrong?" asked the kind Viv. She laid the sympathy on a little too thick, I thought, but that's Viv.

"I've never felt so terrible," said Mr Dropo. "I feel terrible. Oh, I don't feel well at all."

"You're feeling ill?" asked the solicitous Viv.

"Terrible," he said.

Sympathy is sympathy, I thought, and a kid's dad is a kid's dad. But boring is also boring. I decided that if Mr Dropo said terrible one more time, it was the french fry shack for me. I could feel about a kilogram of change in my pocket. I'd checked out the couch before Feet went to bed there the night before.

"Mr Dropo, what's wrong?"

This was Feet's voice. It was about as soft and nurse-like as a pair of garden shears. Feet was playing Bad Cop Kid to Viv's Good Cop Kid.

"Gfhhuugnn. I drank alcohol last night. Whisky. I went to the neighbourhood pub and drank glasses and glasses of whisky. It didn't taste good, but the longer I stayed there drinking whisky the more wonderful the people around me became."

"You've got a hangover?" asked the lovely Viv. She actually placed her cool slender hand on Mr Dropo's forehead.

"It's terrible," said Mr Dropo.

All of a sudden he got up and ran over behind a chestnut tree. Then he came back. His eyes looked as if they had seen sudden death for the thousandth time. He sat carefully down on the park bench. Viv sat beside him. Feet rolled her eyes.

"That's a shame, Mr Dropo," said Viv. "You should be at home, lying down. That's what my uncle Max does when he has a hangover. Except he always lies down on our couch."

"I have never had a hangover before," said Mr Dropo.

We all looked at each other. Besides the advice about your family dog, we kids always said this about Mr Dropo: you should be in his path when he's coming home from the neighbourhood pub, because he always likes to give whatever money he still has in his pockets to the cute kids he encounters on his way home.

"Mr Dropo, that is a little hard to believe," said the Bad Cop Kid.

"I am not Mr Dropo," he said.

I cocked my ear. I was expecting to hear some NaNaNaNa music, indicating suspense and a touch of the supernatural. If we *were* in a movie, I wanted the music and all.

No music. All right, I decided. We were in a book.

"Just kidding," I said aloud.

"What?"

"What?"

"Pardon?"

"Just thinking out loud," I said.

Mr. Dropo now had his head up straight and his eyes open. Feet was standing right in front of him, looking hard at his face.

"Excuse me," she said, "but would you repeat that?"

"Terrible, I feel terrible."

"No, the last thing you said."

"Oh. I am not Mr Dropo."

"You look a lot like him," said Harry, turning his girl

guide hat around backward and looking carefully at the man who might not be Mr Dropo.

"So do three of my friends," said the man on the bench.

We all looked at each other again. Comprehension was sinking in. Feet took a step backward. So did I. Harry took two steps backward. Viv jumped up from the bench and took three steps forward. No one felt at all as if this might all be in a book. Not even a dream. I saw Harry pinch himself hard on the thigh. I had seen him do that before. He did that when he wished with all his heart that he was home in bed asleep with his sleeping cap on.

There was an overall silence for a few moments. If we had wanted to we could have heard people yelling on the beach, but I don't think any of us heard anything. We were all waiting for someone else to say something. The longer we went the more certain I was that I would have to be the person who did it. Why me? I asked silently, I'm just a kid. I should be doing something stupid on a bicycle, not trying to start conversation with an alien creature.

"Are you an alien creature?" I asked.

Mr Dropo, or rather the creature who was not Mr Dropo, looked at me uncomprehendingly.

"Creature?"

"Well," I said, "I guess I mean person. Sort of."

"Alien person?" he or it repeated.

If pressed I would have had to agree that that phrase would not cover the situation. I was wishing that Viv would butt in the way she usually did. I was wishing I would hear my mother yelling furiously at me about coming for supper. It was ten in the morning. I looked at my friends for help. Harry was looking intensely at the toes of his shoes. Viv was staring straight at something directly behind my head. Feet was scrutinizing something she had just taken out of her ear. My friends.

"We, I mean us kids, the four of us," I said. "We have a kind of theory, you might call it, that there has been an invasion of extra parents from another world."

"Another galaxy," said the person on the bench. He looked more calm now, or something like that. He looked as if he was starting to forget about his hangover. That could be good news or bad news, I realized.

"Another galaxy?" Harry suddenly asked. "In some of my favourite movies people in silly suits go from galaxy to galaxy, but how can actual creatures or persons or whatever go that far without dying of old age on the way?"

I was amazed at Harry's volubility. It was an amazing story in itself.

"Old age is a relative concept," said the person who looked like Mr Dropo. "Suppose you take a little Aprilfly into orbit with you. How many generations of Aprilflies will there have been when you come back to Earth a year later?"

"Mayfly," I said.

"Whatever."

Harry's face registered the transmission of an idea. Whenever that happened, I was always glad to be there. He seemed too busy thinking to be scared now.

"You could be hundreds of years old, eh? I mean sort of like dogs living seven years every human year, only more so."

"Mayflies," said Feet.

"Years, well what are years?" said the Mr Dropo-like visitor.

"Holy smoke!" said Harry.

The person, or man, the visiting parent, now took a small package of lozenges from his pants pocket and popped one onto his tongue. He silently offered them around, but we didn't take any. He put the package back into his pocket, and leaned back on the bench with his arms stretched along the top of the backrest. By the time he spoke we were all leaning forward a little.

"I don't know how I got started telling you all this," the man said. "It probably started with the alcohol. We have alcohol in our galaxy but no one there ever thought of drinking it."

"Do you smoke?" asked Feet.

"No one ever thought of that, either. Putting something in your mouth and lighting it on fire—who would ever imagine such a thing?"

"The idea never occurred to you?" asked Viv.

"We *are* ideas," said the artificial Mr Dropo.

Then he disappeared from sight.

We took the bus down to the Vancouver *Moon* building. Boy, were we lucky! Besides us there was just one other group on the bus. This group consisted of two boys, about ten and eleven, and their six parents.

I thought the bus driver might stop with a big hiss of brakes and throw them all off the bus. It happened to me and my friends once, and all we had been doing was singing old time popular songs. Maybe a little too loudly.

This family was not singing. The two kids were yelling and crying, and the parents were speaking calmly, so calmly that I almost wanted to start screaming myself. I saw Harry pull his hat down over his eyes and slump right down in his seat so that he was almost on the floor.

"I don't *want* to go to the dentist!" hollered one kid. "I went to the dentist last week!"

He banged his head on the window beside him, four times.

"I went to the dentist already *this* week!" yelled his brother.

One of the mothers then spoke with a calm voice.

"Now it's *good* that you show resistance to my decision about your life. It shows that you are developing a healthy self-identity," she said, almost cooing. She smoothed the kid's hair with her hand.

"Does that mean I don't have to go?" asked the kid, through a gulp of tears and other head fluids.

"Of course not. You are going to the dentist."

The kids both started waving their arms around. They started chanting: "Don't want to go. Don't want to go."

"That's right, express your anger," said another mother. "Don't bottle it up inside you. Expressing your anger is healthy."

"Clears out the system," added one of the fathers.

"That's stupid, stupid, stupid," yelled the younger son.

"Ah, a healthy scepticism," said another father, calmly. "That is a sign that you are successfully negotiating the maturing process."

I wanted to yell stupid, stupid, stupid, too.

Viv whispered in my ear. I could have heard her from across the street.

"Can you tell which ones are the real parents?"

"No, I can't, and I have been trying," I replied. "Maybe the real parents are still at home."

Feet reached out and touched the bare arm of one of the mothers.

"Excuse me," she said.

"Perfectly all right," the woman said, calmly. "You should not be discouraged in your natural curiosity."

The two kids screamed louder.

"Feels normal to me," Feet whispered to us.

"We have four more stops to go," said Viv, always the bringer of good news.

"I just won't get off the bus," whined one of the sons.

"Neither will I," whined the other, and he linked arms with his brother.

"That's very nice," said one of the mothers. "It shows that you are forming life-long bonds with your sibling."

"Exactly," said a man who may have been her husband. "In one's formative years the ties of the family unit prcparc one's personality for the great adventure that lies waiting in the greater family of humankind."

Feet and Viv and Harry and I decided to get off the bus two stops early and walk the rest of the way.

I had been to the *Moon* building only once before. When I was nine years old my father took me for a tour of the whole works. I remember the press room with the paper zipping around overhead, and I remember the loading ramp where all the little *Moon* trucks lined up to get filled with bales of newspapers. For a year or so, and even a little bit now, I wanted to be a newspaper truck driver. I guess it was interesting to imagine bringing the news to eager and scared readers, but mainly I liked to imagine dumping off a bale of newspapers at each little grocery store along my route, yelling a hello to the people working there. I always imagined I would get a grocery store route, not a newspaper-box route.

I thought every time I drove my empty truck under the

building and up to the loading ramp I would say, "Here I am, the man in the *Moon.*"

Here I was back with three other members of my film review club, on business this time.

Speaking of film reviews and the *Moon,* of course we always read the reviews written by Andrew Marx. Andrew Marx reviews every movie that comes to the commercial theatres in town. He does not seem to have any cinema theory. As far as we can tell, he does not read the European cinema magazines you can find in the racks at Flics Cafe. But he has his own personal taste. He is a big fan of teenage horror movies. He really warms up when he gets to write about *Guillotine on Maple Street III* or *Beach Party Bloodbath IV.* I can't remember his review of *Spilled Intestines VI.* I think he called it a minor classic. I never did finish *my* review of it. We four junior reviewers seldom went to that kind of movie. Well, Harry did, but we wouldn't let him write reviews of them. There aren't really any movies that Harry won't go to. He even goes to see movies starring that short guy who tears his shirt off and yells "Yo!" and runs through flames carrying a huge machine gun.

Anyway, here we were at the *Moon,* cooling our heels in a little reception area that had copies of this morning's edition on all handy surfaces.

"We would like to see the editor," Viv had said.

"Which editor?" asked the woman with the earphones on her head.

"I don't know. The main editor," said Viv. She stood

with her fists on her hips, to show that she might be related to Concerned Parent, who always writes angry letters to the editor.

"Please wait, and I will see what I can do," said the earphones woman.

We were all pretty excited about being in the big newspaper building, and I suppose we were somewhat scared waiting for the main editor. But we all sort of sprawled in our orange chairs, to show that this was just the normal way a bunch of movie critics might spend their day.

I, for one, jumped a little when the woman poked her head through the door and announced that Mr Boudreau would be with us in just a minute. She did not have earphones on now.

I knew the name Boudreau, of course. My father called him Mr Booboo around our house. My father was one of those men fated to spend their lives working for people they perceived to be less intelligent than themselves. I figured that he was probably right. It must not be very nice to have a father you don't think is smarter than average.

Mr Boudreau came in and motioned us to remain seated. Harry got all tangled up trying to remain seated while he was standing up. He yanked his hat off his head and held it in his lap. How do kids learn the last scraps of polite posture in these days, I wondered.

Mr Boudreau sat down and hinched his chair forward a little. I could see right away that he was one of those guys who had taken a course in public relations. If he was an insurance salesman he would be calling you by your first name and using it in every sentence.

"Now what can I do for you ladies and gentlemen?" he asked.

"Actually, we're just kids," said Feet.

I glared at her. She gave me her blank-eyed glance. I thought that I had better fill in any potholes here.

"Well," I said, trying to think of a way to keep Mr Boudreau from thinking we were nuts, "we know about a big story that's been taking place in town for the last couple of days, and there hasn't been anything about it in the paper."

"You don't say." He was all ready to humour us. "I would be grateful if you would fill me in. We at the *Moon* feel a responsibility to keep our citizens informed."

I knew how my father felt. I wanted to walk out of there right then. But I knew this was probably a rare event–getting an editor's time and attention.

"These are my friends," I said, indicating the other three. "Harry Fieldstone, Viv Lemieux, and Miss Cilantry Corbishly."

Feet shot me her most dangerous look. I was going to have to watch my back afterward. Mr Boudreau nodded to them all.

"And I'm Neville Neatby. I'm Denton Neatby's son."

"Who's he?"

"He works here."

"Oh, I see. Well, what is this story you have for me?"

"Curiously enough, it has to do with parents too," I said,

making it sound as if I were Mr Boudreau's equal or even colleague.

"Aha. We usually cover just about everything on the subject in our Lifestyles Section."

"This has to do with parents from outer space," I said.

I had delivered my best passing shot. Let's see him return that one, I thought. I could feel my friends admiring me.

"Oh yes, the alien moms and dads. We are running a story on that in this evening's edition."

I did not like Mr Booboo's smile at all.

"What?"

"What?"

"What?"

"Pardon?"

Mr Boudreau got up and poked his head and upper body around the door.

"Fiona, give me the late edition, will you?"

He re-emerged holding the thin Tuesday *Moon* with blurry colour pictures on the front page. With that special way newspaper people have with handling a newspaper, he opened it to a back page in the third section, and folded the paper so that a story on the bottom of the page became the centre of attention.

UNUSUAL STORY RELATED BY SEVERAL OFF-SPRING.

That was the headline.

The story started: "Some younger residents of the west side have been reporting an influx of undesirable relatives.

In accounts that might have been lifted from the pages of a supermarket tabloid..."

"There's your problem," I said.

"I have a problem?" asked Mr Boudreau, looking at his watch. It was one of those massive watches with gadgets all over it. He could probably push a button and check the temperature of the pool at the Bombay Hilton.

"Well, look at the headline," I said. "That's the worst headline I have ever seen."

"What would you have written if you were writing the headline?" asked Mr Boudreau. He was even more patronizing now.

"I would have written the same thing as my father would have written: PARENTS FROM SPACE."

Guido brought us our stuff and smiled fondly at us, a great big Ukrainian smile that threatened to segment his head. Usually Guido's smile could make me happy for an hour or more. Now I glumly stirred the white stuff into my cappuccino. I saw that Feet and Viv were doing the same thing. Harry was looking deep down into his bottle of Tahiti Treat. The four of us had our elbows on the table and our chins in our hands. Three of us used our right hands for the purpose. I used my left.

"Well, so much for that," I said.

No one said anything for a while. We could hear Guido sigh heavily. He was across the room, looking at an old cinema magazine on the counter. He had his right elbow on the counter and his chin in his right hand. There were no other customers in Flics.

"What that?" asked Feet.

I was too discouraged to elaborate. I thought she knew what I was referring to, and she just wanted to express her own frustration somehow. So she picked on my demonstrative pronoun.

"That that," I said.

"What about that that?" she asked.

"I am just saying that that that should have been obvious."

Harry stared at us blankly, his head turning from one to another as we spoke.

"Let your feelings out, Nev," said Viv.

Harry, with the help of his Tahiti Treat, let out a big ugly burp.

"Not you, you idiot," said Feet.

"I am not an idiot," said Harry. "I have been upgraded to moron."

"This is getting us nowhere," I said.

"We were supposed to be going somewhere?" asked Feet.

I think she was practicing to be a married person. Or a

mother. At least she didn't tell adult jokes. I would have given up on life if she had said "I'll nowhere you."

I noticed that for a few moments Viv had been running her finger around the inside of my empty cappuccino cup, getting the last of the white stuff. This was partly to let me know that in the middle of any great crisis she would remain calm. This from the girl who usually jumps two meters in the air if someone snaps his bubble gum.

"Listen, you guys," I said.

"And others," said Feet.

"Listen, everyone, I said. We are just kids, right?"

"Yes and no," said Viv.

"Maybe we should get some advice from a grownup-type person," I said.

"A parent?" asked Viv at what would have been the top of most people's voices. "How do we tell them from aliens or alienettes?"

"No, no," I said, signalling that we should keep our voices down. "I am thinking of a regular grownup who isn't a parent. I'm thinking of Guido." I lifted my eyebrows and jiggled my head toward our innkeeper across the room.

"Isn't he a parent?" asked Viv, in a shrieking whisper.

"Isn't it apparent?" I responded. "If he were a parent, could he afford to run this nice but stupid coffee house?"

"Neville is right," said Harry.

"How would you know, you moron?" said Feet.

She didn't mean it as an insult. She just couldn't resist taking note of Harry's promotion.

I guess you could say that of the four of us, Feet is the

most socially conscious as they say, but she is also from the fanciest address. Those things seem to go together, or so it seems in my limited experience.

"Here's my plan," I said, and then we all put our heads close together and went buzz buzz buzz for a little bit. When we all sat back we had half-satisfied, half-expectant little pre-smiles on our faces. Harry, for instance, looked the way he always looked just before the lights went down at the Smedley Theatre.

"Guido, can we ask your advice on something?" enquired Viv, teenage sincerity radiating from her face.

Guido does not necessarily trust us. We are teenagers, after all. But he likes us because we are often in his place buying something to drink, though we tend to hang over an empty cup or glass for a long time. He doesn't dislike us because, though we are teenagers, we don't make a lot of brainless noise, and we don't put our shoes on the furniture.

He looked up from his magazine and smiled a junior version of his face-splitting smile. It would have been the perfect smile for a Ukrainian travel poster.

"We serve and protect," he said.

"What?"

"Pardon?"

"Shoot," he said.

"Well," said Viv. "Suppose you were making a movie, see, and it's about these kids who stumble on a secret invasion from another planet."

"Galaxy," said Harry.

"Okay," said Viv. "Now here's the problem—"

"In the script," I said.

"Yeah," said Viv. "The kids know there's an invasion on, but the grownups won't take it seriously. They think it's just these kids' imagination. They think these kids have been seeing too many movies. Well, here's the other problem: some of the grownups know about it because *they* are the invaders."

Guido's smile grew larger and larger. His eyebrows rose into the wrinkles in his forehead.

"Wasn't that one on Channel Forty-One the other night?" he suggested.

"No, no," said Viv. "This is an original script by us four."

"Maybe you should stick to *reviewing* movies," suggested Guido.

"That wasn't the advice we were looking for," said Feet.

"Okay, shoot," said Guido.

I figured he meant shoot as in filming a movie rather than shoot as in instructing a firing squad.

"We want to know how the four kids, uh, save the world. How can they get the invaders to leave the planet?"

"Why don't you have the army zap them with flame throwers and ray guns?" suggested Guido.

"So we can have a close-up of some army general saying Good Lord, it just bounces off them?" said Feet, a snake of irony in her words.

"Say, that's not a bad idea," said Harry.

"Harry, your instructions are to shut up," said Viv.

Guido took off his little pocket-apron and made a few wipes at the counter top. Then he put it down and walked over to join us. He pulled up a chair from a nearby table and sat in it backward, as in all the movies from the forties.

"Here's my advice," he said.

"Shoot," said Viv.

Guido was enjoying this. It was the first time we had ever asked him for advice. I mean here were these four veteran film reviewers, sophisticates of the cafe scene, and now they were deferring to Guido Padrobenko, humble tapsman of Kaiser Street.

"If you ask me, I think you are making a mistake. I don't think the kids in your movie should turn against the creatures from outer space. Why? Because kids themselves are from outer space."

None of us uttered a sound in response.

"Now, now, don't interrupt me," said Guido. "Why do I say that kids are from outer space? Well, one day they do not exist, and then before you know it, there they are, popping out of their earthly hosts. An invasion from outer space, if you ever saw one."

Harry's eyes lit up. He took off his girl guide hat and put it on the table in front of him.

"It's like *The Night of the Triffids*," he exclaimed, "starring Edmund Keel."

(I hope you understand he meant *The* Day *of the Triffids*, and *Howard* Keel.)

"Yes, as far as I can see, kids come from outer space. That's why human beings can't understand half of what they're saying," Guido continued.

"I don't feel as if I came from outer space," I said. "I feel like an Earth kid. I would want to fight any invasion from outer space."

"Then make sure no one ever has a baby," said Guido.

"Hear hear," said Feet.

Guido got up and went back to the counter. We looked at each other absently. If we were making a movie about an invasion of the babies from outer space, Guido's advice would have earned a screen credit. We could call him puppet master or something. Not key grip.

Now Guido arrived back at our table with a tray of drinks, some kind of fairly thick brownish-red liquid in five tall glasses.

"What's this?" asked Viv.

"A drink from outer space," said Guido.

It was Harry, of course, who ventured first. He took a swig, frowned, smiled, and took another swig.

"I don't know what it is, but it's terrific," he said.

Guido pulled up his backward chair again.

"Now," he said, "about this business of teenagers from space. Do you happen to subscribe to the Big Bong Theory for the creation of the universe?"

"Big Bang," said Feet dryly.

"Whatever. I was reading the February issue of *Science Trivia* magazine, where it was pointed out that all the stuff inside a human body is also found all through the universe and then some. According to this, we are all fragments of the Big Bong, so we all came from outer space, anyway."

We were all silent for a while, except for the odd glug of brown liquid here and there.

"I guess you got us there, Guido," said Harry.

Normally the four of us would break up around the middle of the day and head for our individual houses for lunch. But no one felt much like going home. So we drifted through the middle of the day, kind of gooping around the street and the park and the beach. It was a nice day at Kannegeiser Beach. There were middling-grey clouds in the sky and something that looked like rain against the side of the mountain. This meant that there weren't many people leaning up against the driftwood logs in the grey sand.

Normally I hate the beach. I even shudder a little when I see the traditional crowded beach picture on the front page of the *Moon* every year when the first sunny warm spell occurs. For one thing it is hard to read at the beach. The bright sun shines off the paper. Wind blows the pages around. Sand gets between them. And you can't find a comfortable position to read in. If you do, there will be a wet dog shaking itself nearby, even if it's illegal to take a dog to the beach. Or there will be some dorks with portable radios turned up high. Have you ever noticed that the dorks who take their electronic blasters to the beach or drive around the streets with their car stereos up to the maximum always have the very worst taste in music?

No, the beach is generally a terrible place. Except for the fish and chips huts. For some reason the best fish and chips are to be found at the beach. They taste like the fish and chips in England used to taste when you bought them wrapped up in a newspaper. At least that's what my father told me every time he took me to the beach when I was smaller. One year they introduced pre-frozen french fries to the beach huts, and the people rose in thunderous reproach. That's what it said in the *Moon*. There was a photo of a deserted beach hut with a lonely fry-cook leaning on the counter.

THEY CASHED IN THEIR CHIPS, said my father's headline.

But other than those fish and chips the beach is a miserable place. I know that a lot of people claim to enjoy it, but I figure that makes sense. Have you ever noticed the kind of people you see enjoying themselves at the beach? Either they are lying sprawled out with unconscious cow expressions on their faces, or they are engaged in some kind of low grade imitation of the mindless activities encountered in beer commercials on television. If you stand up at a crowded beach and survey the collection of human specimens, you can't go away with a very high hope for the planet.

I mean if I want to go swimming I will head for a pool, preferably one that little kids haven't been relaxing their bladders in. At the beach you have to make sure you are not stepping on some tattooed dork's broken beer bottle on your way into the water. Then after you come out you can't get to your towel and stuff without getting sand stuck all over you, especially between your last two toes. I hate having cold wet sand between my last two toes. Then even if you make it to your towel, you still have a wet bathing suit clamped around the middle of your body.

Meanwhile some idiots are shouting the most offensive words they can think of because they know the mothers are worried about their little kids hearing them. These are the same guys who go to football games and shout obscenities at the visiting team.

But this was not a normal day at the beach. It was fairly warm but dull and grey. We were not there to throw frisbees or splash each other. There were only about two dozen other people on the sand, and half of them were just punks who had found a place to take a rest from petty crime.

Down near the volleyball net we could see a family of eight. There were two children and six grownups who all resembled one another more than usual. Of course.

None of us got fish but all of us got chips. We splattered vinegar on them and shook salt on them. Then we sat in a circle on the sand and stuck the chips one by one into our mouths. Nobody said anything till the last chip had gone into the last mouth, Viv's as usual.

Then we started talking about our main concern.

"Here's what I can't stop thinking about," said Feet.

"How come we all have this parents problem except for Neville?"

"I have a parents problem," I said.

"You know what I mean," said Feet, and then she sighed loudly.

"What's different about Neville?" asked Viv.

"He has very large ears that stick out," suggested Feet.

I really hate to have my ears become a topic of conversation. I have tried everything for them. When I was a little kid my mother taped them back. Later I wore my hair every way I could think of. I make a practice of talking to people without facing them directly. My mother has stopped promising me that they will quit sticking out when I get older. People I don't even know call me "Sails".

Even if they protected me against extra parents from outer space I wouldn't feel comfortable with my ears.

"He plays the tuba," said Viv. "Who would volunteer to live with that?"

The tuba isn't all that bad. I play the double B-flat tuba in the junior band, because I didn't run fast enough when Mr. Tchicai the music teacher was looking for a new bass player to replace the kid who had graduated to the senior band. The only thing I really don't like about the tuba is polishing it before a parade or a basketball game. Jody Love likes to finish polishing her piccolo and then hang around gloating while I smear the Brasso on my horn.

But when we do Colonel Bogie, I pound out those bass notes and for a while no one can hear a piccolo or any other instrument.

"One of his eyes is bigger than the other one," said Viv.

"His Nikes smell worse than most," said Feet.

"Could be I'm so intelligent that aliens are intimidated by me?" I put in.

"If you are so intelligent how come you wound up playing the tuba?" asked Viv.

Feet all at once gave Harry a swat on the shoulder.

"You haven't said anything to help us out," she said gruffly. "All you want is a free ride here. You had your chips. Now contribute."

Harry pretended he was musing hard. He looked out to sea and squinted. He put his forefinger against the tip of his chin. He took off his girl guide hat and ran his knuckles back and forth on the top of his head.

"Neville is the only one who is left-handed," he said.

"Get serious," said Viv.

"Come on, Harry, try to think," said Feet.

No one knew exactly when it started to rain. I looked around and saw that everyone else had left the beach. The four of us had Kannegeiser all to ourselves, except for the pigeons that were obviously wondering whether we had left any chips in our cardboard dishes. It never did rain very hard but the small raindrops got closer and closer together. Harry put his hat back on. Viv's red hair was a little plastered to her skull. I had to look over the tops of my glasses. Feet lay down flat on her back in the sand and let the rain fall on her.

Passers-by might think this was a disturbed group of children.

My parents were always telling me to count my blessings. I was reminded once a day how lucky I was to be living in a nice house on Bicuspid Avenue instead of a back alley in some dirty oily corner of some city in a country where they don't have microwave ovens. When I was four years old they said eat your spaghetti, think about the starving kids on some other continent who would love to have a plate of spaghetti, even with store-bought spaghetti sauce on it. I hated spaghetti, still do. I would rather eat sardines than spaghetti.

When a parent says think about the starving kids in some place, any kid naturally replies that he will gladly give up his stuff for them. It is one of those situations you would think a parent would remember and avoid. Parents always say they know what you're trying to pull on them because they were kids themselves. But when they don't know the answer to the starving kids in whatsis, you have to wonder.

I really would have liked to give my food to starving kids on another continent, and when I get to be an adult or even a parent, I am going to remember those kids. I don't know whether my parents think about them very often. Maybe they do.

Anyway, when I considered the problems of kids with parents from another galaxy, I counted my blessings.

My main blessing was that I had only one father and one mother and one sister. I think that if I had some more copies of my grandmother, I would follow their advice and be the champion juvenile delinquent she calls me. I wondered whether any of those parents from outer space were also grandparents.

I mean imagine a house with three or four of my mothers in it. There would be about eight cigarettes going at once. The smoke would be so thick you wouldn't be able to see across the living room. Every ashtray would be piled up like a slag heap and spilling out all over the place. We would all be gasping with our heads out the windows. Here is what they would say if I said, "I think I will skip dessert and go for a piece of carrot cake at Guido's."

"I'll skip dessert you."

"I'll carrot cake you."

"I'll Guido you."

It would probably be easier with a few extra versions of my father, though the silence might get under my skin. There they would be, sitting in our easy chairs and on the couch, coughing quietly and reading *Caboose News* and *The Railroad Earth*.

But here is what puzzled me: obviously one set of those parents would be the original ones, the authentic ones. The same principle would apply in other people's houses. How come those original parents didn't assert their priority?

It didn't take me long to figure out the answer to that one. The foreign creatures were such accurate copies that their claims would be just as likely-sounding. Probably there had been a fight at first in each household with alien visitors. Then the real parents had seen that their claims were no more convincing than any others. Most kids think their parents are from another world, anyway.

Maybe, I thought, if there was a happy ending to this story, if the extra parents left for another planet all at once, they would take the earth-born ones with them.

Then I thought again, and what I thought was no no no.

So I was kind of lucky, living in such an uncrowded house. My sister, of course, couldn't be bothered about the situation.

"Big deal," she said. "There's always something from outer space."

As far as she was concerned I didn't exist, anyway, so for her the house was even less crowded than it was for me. But having just one set of parents was a kind of luxury, I told myself. So I owed it to my friends to see whether they could stay over again.

"We're not running a boarding school," said my father.

"Shh," I replied. I didn't want the kids in the other room to hear such a remark.

If he had said yes or nothing, my mother would have refused outright. Now she was a little thrown off. She blew cigarette smoke out of her nostrils and waved it away from her face with her free hand.

"They will have to phone their parents and get permission," she said. Then she turned to my father, who was trying to figure out how the coffee machine works. "It *is* the summer holidays," she pointed out.

"You're right, it *are* a lovely night in June."

For a headline writer he had a lot of interest in grammar.

So of course you know what happened. They all phoned their parents or at least some kind of parents, and all of them were instructed to come home. Harry asked whether he could bring me overnight, and got permission, but I refused to go. Feet asked whether she could bring Viv, and Viv asked whether she could bring Feet, and they both got permission, but they both received sincere instructions to come home.

Never before had we been forced to consider so carefully the principle of one-family dwellings.

That night, after my parents had finished observing this week's re-run of the adventures of the neurotic policemen in Pittsburgh, I glommed onto the television news, some of which was advice about which automobile to buy and which lawn-fertilizer to use.

Actually, I watch the news quite a lot in the summer, when my parents are less excited about my bedtime. I am a fan of air crashes. It's crazy, probably. You get all excited when you hear the announcer say, "A Turkish jumbo jet with 340 people aboard..." and then you feel horrible, and flinch and throw your hands up in front of your face, and shake your head hard, because the TV camera in your head sees those upside-down mountains coming. And there are really small kids in those planes, and flying was not their idea. They were just brought on board by their parents.

Weren't we all? Weren't we all? Hostages to our fate on Space Ship Earth. That was not the name of any recent science fiction movie. Recent science fiction movies were all about muscular guys with heavy weapons making bright red explosions in someone else's architecture.

My mind was wandering, as it tends to do while I'm watching television. It is a living mind's *duty* when television is on. One of the saddest things I have ever seen is the waiting room at my dentist's office. My dentist has made it all high tech and user-friendly. He has a bank of television screens on the wall, with headphones you can clamp on your head. He has a choice of tapes for the kids to watch, things like puppets and flashing numbers, and animal cartoons in which only one hand moves for a while, and so on. Here is the sad part: I look into that waiting room and see about eight little kids staring empty-eyed at the television screens, speakers clamped on their heads. And sadder yet: their mothers are sitting in that room, too, and they don't see anything wrong.

Anyway, my mind was trying to escape while my body was lying on the floor of our TV room and my brain was holding my eyes still, looking at the screen. Let me out of here, my mind was thinking. Take me with you, my body was whispering.

Then we all came back, because the invasion of the parents was on television at last.

Mackenzie MacDonald, the anchorman on CJNK, had been talking about "unconfirmed reports" for a while.

"...and because there have been no complaints of actual criminal or civil wrongdoing, the city's police force has not been engaged in any investigative activity."

Well, you can change that into regular English and understand it pretty well. Now there was a scene on the lawn outside a brick building where one man was holding a microphone near another man's nose.

"Dr. Hosenklappe, you people at the university must be pretty excited when reports such as these begin to circulate. What has your response been and what are your plans?"

That was the reporter's eager question. Dr. Hosenklappe was wearing a white lab coat and holding an unlit pipe in his hand, which he used to point at things, pick at his ear, clench between his teeth for a few seconds, push against his cheek, and so on. He did all these things while giving his answer.

"Well, I cannot zpeak for the rest of the university, but here in the psychology department we are pretty used to these things, ezpecially out here among the student population. Mass hysteria, ezpecially in the zummer, does not zurprise us. Does not surprise us, that is."

"Then you think the stories of extra parents are some kind of mental phenomenon?"

"No question about it. The fact that these youngsters chose parents as their invaders from outer space would suggest that they are unwittingly delivering to us the diagnosis. I mean they could have zuffered, I mean suffered, an invasion of dogs from outer space, or giraffes, or electric can-openers..."

"Dr. Hosenklappe, what do you say to a teenage boy who is afraid to go home because he is going to face demands for twenty hours of chores, let us say?"

"...or kimonos, or volleyball players, or stethoscopes, or guys who wear baseball hats backward, or..."

Now the scene was the inside of another professor's office. There were books and papers and maps and charts all over and under everything. There did not seem to be any place to sit down, so the reporter and the professor were standing beside a file cabinet that had a mountain of open books on top of it.

"Professor Purzelbaum," said the reporter, sticking the microphone near the professor's nose, "we have spoken to a member of the psychology department who dismisses the claims of mass parenthood as a kind of collective delusion. Do you in the astronomy department have another view?"

Professor Purzelbaum was also wearing a lab coat, but his was unbuttoned and had the collar turned up. There were stains of several different colours on it. I wondered why an astronomer or astronomy professor would wear a lab coat. It's not as if astronomy were a laboratory science. Of course I knew a kid who wore a lab coat all the time. I think he slept in his lab coat. It looked as if Professor Purzelbaum slept in his lab coat, too. Maybe he was the father of the kid I knew. But the kid was named John Judd. Maybe that was a fake name. It certainly sounded like one. It sounded like the kind of name a teenage rock and roll guitar player would make up for himself. I wondered what kind of music name I would make up for myself. Maybe something foreign-sounding, like Prosper Yamamoto. I could double on the koto.

This is how a person's mind wanders when television is on, even when the subject is close to his heart. The heart of Prosper Yamamoto.

"We in the astronomy department have several different views," said Professor Purzelbaum, if that was his real name. "My own is not necessarily shared by other members of the department."

Professor Purzelbaum had a head that was shaped like Sugarloaf Mountain in Rio de Janeiro. He had yellowish-brown hair that sprouted on the top of the mountain and hung down on every side. His ears stuck out through the cascade of hair, one on each side. He looked like an Earthling, but he didn't overdo it.

"But your view, your personal view, is not that of the psychology department," persisted the reporter.

Professor Purzelbaum had an old pair of black-rimmed glasses on his long bumpy nose, which protruded through the cascade of hair on the front side of his head. The bridge of the glasses was held together by adhesive tape. The rectangular lens on one side was lower than the one on the other side.

"Certainly different from the fellow you mentioned, who spoke of mass frenzy."

"Hysteria, he called it. A psycho-medical term, I believe," said the reporter.

"Hmm, ahem, yes, well, exactly, I suppose, uh huh," suggested the professor.

The camera shifted so that it was behind Professor Purzelbaum's head for a moment. There was nothing sticking out through the cascade of hair on that side. The reporter was nodding his head. The way Professor Purzelbaum's jaw was moving did not seem to match the words I could hear him saying. Watch interviews on the news: that always happens. I guess they go and take that second angle once per interview to show that their correspondent is really paying attention.

"So, what is your position?" asked the reporter, off camera again. "Do you think there really is some sort of extraterrestrial invasion?"

Professor Purzelbaum looked around his jumbled office

for a moment, and then picked up a meter-long pointer. As he talked he pointed at various things that did not have anything to do with what he was saying. At first the camera followed his gestures. Then it just returned to his face. The last pointed-at thing the camera looked at was a little paperback book called *Time Travellers Strictly Cash*. I missed some of what Professor Purzelbaum was saying, because this time my mind was wandering around stuff the television was showing right in front of my face. Television just finds more and more ways to make me jumpy. I always wish that the teachers in school didn't try to attract our attention by showing us stuff on television. It just makes me suspicious. Oops, there goes my mind again. Anyway, I picked up Professor Purzelbaum's answer in mid-flight.

"...very unlikely that they could have got here in the flesh, if flesh is what they have at home, and then somehow converted it into human flesh, you might say parent flesh. No, I think it is more likely that they found a way to travel that is faster than the speed of light, because that is what they would need unless they are the tenth generation of people, or whatever they are, who went through a kind of generational mini-history aboard ship. Unless they have lifetimes that equal a thousand of ours, so that what we consider to be a hundred years is just an hour or so to them. But no, I rather lean—"

Here the professor leaned to his left.

"—to the theory that they travelled across the deep reaches of space, if that is what has happened, as ideas, as thoughts."

Aha, I thought. This guy is nearly as smart as my friend Harry Fieldstone.

The reporter put on his wrapping-up voice.

"So you and Professor Hosenklappe both attribute the reports of interstellar invaders to immaterial mind activity."

Professor Purzelbaum's eyes could be seen to open wider behind a fringe of yellowish-brown hair and above his crooked spectacles.

"I guess you could put it that way," he said.

As Mackenzie MacDonald, the anchorman, went on to discuss another beautiful downtown building that was going to be blown to smithereens, I kept the image of Professor Purzelbaum between the big eye and my little ones. I couldn't get over the fact that he had agreed with Harry, who is definitely not a moron, by the way, despite his idiosyncrasies.

I thought it would be an interesting idea for us to go out and pay him a visit. Maybe I would ask him why he wore a lab coat. Maybe we would ask him whether he had any kids.

13.

I called a special meeting of the club the next day. We gathered at ten in the morning at Guido's, and while three of us had sensible beverages and one had a banana-lime cocktail, I told them about the professors on TV. Viv had seen the beginning of the news item, but one of her mothers had turned off the set when Dr Hosenklappe called the space visitors a mass hysteria.

"Hmmph," this mother had said.

At least she hadn't said "I'll mass hysteria *him*."

Guido put free doughnut holes down in front of us. One each.

"Anything from outer space today?" he asked.

Feet tried to give him a withering stare, but she was putting the doughnut hole into her mouth at the same time and it didn't work. Just in case Harry was going to snicker, she took his welder's cap off and smote him alongside the head with it.

"Anything from out of the deeps this morning?" asked Guido. He was picking his teeth with the plastic toothpick from his Swiss army knife. What a neat parent he would have made. But he was the only adult Ukrainian I ever met who wasn't married with energetic kids.

"You are thinking of *Star Dreck*," said Viv, shaking her red hair. "What we have is a real human problem."

"Well, sort of human," said Harry.

"No, I mean real human trouble," said Viv, banging her hand on the table. She was shooting glances every fifteen seconds at the street outside.

"Remember Burt Arness in *The Thing*," said Harry. "He was a human problem, but he was really a huge broccoli."

Feet reached for the welder's cap, but Harry ducked

away in time. I took advantage of the space made and spoke out in support of Viv. I may have been the only person who had seen her wipe a trickle of thin snot off the corner under her nose.

"It *is* a human problem," I said. "And we are the humans who have it. I have it a lot less than you people do, less than Viv does. My parents are not the best that the planet Earth has to show, but at least there are only two of them."

"I don't even know how I managed to get here this morning," said Viv. "When you phoned I could hear telephones being picked up all over the house."

Guido brought another round of doughnut holes. At moments like this we knew why we liked making our critical headquarters here at Flics.

"I think you should go and see Professor Putzelbottom," he said. "Forget about the other one, if I was you."

We agreed among us. Dr Hosenklappe was to be kept in reserve, in case we needed some psychology. As it was we were more interested in the looniness out there in the real world.

Well, it was real if this wasn't a movie we were in.

"If this is a movie we are acting in," persisted Harry, "how come I cannot see a camera anywhere?"

I sighed perceptibly, nearly putting my shoulders out of joint.

"Listen carefully, Harry. We are not actors making a movie. We are characters in a movie. That's why we can't see the cameras, any more than a character in a book can see the author's typewriter. Do you begin to understand?"

Harry took off his welder's cap and did a perfect imitation of Satch in the old Bowery Boys classics.

"Jeeze, Neville, you told me we were in real life. How can we be movie characters? How can I review movies if I'm *in* a movie? Help me, help me, as that gink said in *The Fly*."

So we all jumped on a noisy smoky gassy bus and rode out to the university. Every once in a while we would see a kid running down the sidewalk or across someone's yard.

It is surprisingly easy to go and see a professor of astronomy, even if he has been on television. You just have to find the physics buildings, and then find the astronomy department, and then look around for a door with his name on it. Actually in this case it had more than DR ROSARIO PURZELBAUM on it. Taped or thumbtacked to the wood were cut-out strips of space comics, a rose that had been dead for a long time, a blue ribbon on which were printed the words FIRST PLACE HUBBARD SQUASH MARYLEBONE AUTUMN FAIR, a newspaper photo of the winner of the annual California ugly dog contest, a completed double acrostic from *Atlantic Monthly*, a handwritten sign that said "I am momentarily in another space-time continuum. Back in five minutes", one dark purple sock, and a lot of other stuff.

The door wasn't locked. It wasn't even closed. It was ajar, or maybe more than that, maybe about five jars. When Harry tried it with his fingers it swung open a little more.

"You know," he said, "under all that other stuff there is probably a sign that says come on in and wait."

"Sure," said Feet, "and maybe another one that says free ice cream and cupcakes."

"I could go for a cupcake right now," said Harry.

"Name a time when you couldn't," said Feet.

But she sidled into the office while she was saying it. Then we all kind of sidled in, not really noticing, you understand, but managing to wind up inside the door rather than in the hall.

The office looked just as it had on the television news, but now we could see it all. There were papers and books and magazines and charts and maps and sandwiches and apple cores and rubber boots and spectacles and empty kleenex boxes and tennis rackets and toothbrushes and cheque books and letter openers and unopened envelopes and dried orange peels and hats and knitted gloves and callipers and chalk sticks and broken umbrellas all over the place. There were also bookshelves full of books and objects in front of the books.

Viv was reading the spines on a shelf behind a heap of stuff that suggested that there might be a desk under it. She whistled and gestured that we should come over and read with her.

She pointed. We were looking at a collection of books

written by Professor Purzelbaum. Here are the titles we saw:

Homeless and Ugly in the Solar System: An Ontological Survey of Irregular Self-Perceptions among Humanoids.

Stepladders on the Moons of Neptune.

Great Scott, It's Alive!: An Illustrated Encyclopedia of Everything That Has Come from Outer Space.

Who's Who in the Galaxy.

Um Antwort Wird Gebeten.

A Cubic Foot at the Other End of the Universe: Einstein for Rookie Carpenters.

À beau mentir qui vient de loin.

Feet hymphed.

"Hymph! If you uneducated louts could read French you would know that we have come to the right place."

"I don't see why we should need to understand French when they have invented subtitles," said Harry. "I could follow everything in this movie if they would only give me subtitles."

"Can you read in a mirror?" I asked.

"What? What for?"

"The subtitles would be in front of you and backward, as if they were in a mirror," I said. "They're set up for the audience to read, not the characters."

"What about Russian subtitles? Their letters are all backward anyway, so we could follow them."

While he was saying this I saw Viv out the side of my eye. She was twisting her body around, as if she were trying to read something that was backward and in front of her.

"We are not in a movie," said Feet decisively. "We have enough problems as it is. We don't need to invent anything."

"Don't take anything for granted; maybe we are all in a movie, and maybe it is a foreign film," said a voice new to all of us but me.

It was Professor Purzelbaum in the doorway. His lab coat had a cleaner's tag safety-pinned to it. He came inside and lifted up his pointer.

"Hymmph," said Feet.

"Don't tell me," said Professor Purzelbaum, holding up his hand, palm toward us. "You are Argentinian exchange students who want to enroll in my Old Men in Moons course in the fall."

He smiled, his hair falling between his eyes and his black-rimmed spectacles.

"Not even close," said Feet, and it was hard to tell whether she was triumphant or truculent.

Good, I got to use that word.

"You are on a treasure hunt and you think there is a map hidden in the frame behind that picture of Isaac Asimov." He used his pointer to tap the wall next to the picture.

"Professor Purzelbaum—"

"Call me Reginald," he said.

"It says Rosario on your door," said Viv.

"Okay, Rosario," said the professor.

I noticed a thin ribbon of suspicion going through the room. Maybe this man was a parent from outer space. But

I dropped that idea quickly. I just figured he was an astronomy professor. And he seemed like a nice person. I place a lot of importance on a nice person.

"We are just a quartet of film critics," said Harry.

"Of course. I was just going to say that," said the Professor.

"With too many parents all of a sudden," said Feet.

"Especially me," said Viv.

"Aha!" said the Professor.

"Neville saw you on television," said Harry.

"I never watch television," said Professor Purzelbaum. "It makes your mind wander."

"Well, Neville says he thinks you are our only chance."

"And a slim one at that," added Feet.

Professor Purzelbaum sniffed and sniffed again. He turned around once, as if looking for something. He shoved his cascading hair up to the top of his sugarloaf head, and it fell down again. A pencil dropped out of it and fell onto a bare part of the floor, where it proceeded to roll under the pile that appeared to be a desk.

"Ah yes, the moms and dads from another galaxy," he said. "I think I am starting to get a grip on that subject."

As he said this he grabbed my shoulder and squeezed it till my arm went numb.

"You believe us?" asked Harry.

"I am a scientist. Scientists do not believe." He whacked his pointer against a pile of student assignments. "We observe!"

"Always?" asked Viv.

"I think so," he said.

Feet followed him around the crowded little room until he came to a relative stillness, and then she stood right in front of him and looked through his drooping hair into the front part of his head.

"Professor–" she started.

"Call me Roderick."

"Rosario," said Viv.

"Yes, that."

"Professor Purzelbaum, will you come with us and have a look at what we have to live with?" asked Feet.

Her voice was a smooth mixture of beseechment and threat. At that moment I was proud of her and scared of her at the same time. She hadn't hit me for a long time, not since grade six. But there are certain arrangements between kids, relationships that were set up some time in their early acquaintanceship. And they never change much. I wonder whether this goes on when the kids get to be grownups, or even parents, heaven forbid!

"Sure," said Professor Purzelbaum.

I thought he would hang his lab coat on a hook and put on his sports jacket or suit top the way the doctor always did in *Magnificent Obsession*.

But he just stepped out with his lab coat on.

"Aren't you going to close the door?" asked Viv, energetically, but with a trace of doubt she had learned in the past ten minutes.

"Sure," said Professor Purzelbaum.

He gave the door a kick. It swung shut, and then it popped open a bit.

And off we went.

You haven't lived till you've had a ride across town in Professor Purzelbaum's car.

Actually, while you are riding across town in Professor Purzelbaum's car, you think about living quite a lot.

I am just a kid, you would say, but I have watched people driving, and I have to say that even my mother and father know more about automobile driving than Professor Purzelbaum does.

Take the gear shift, for instance. Professor Purzelbaum did not seem to believe in sequence. He would just push the gear shift into any position he could, so that sometimes the car would chug along, and Professor Purzelbaum would say "what an *auspuff*", and other times it would jump forward and suddenly stop, as if it had run into an invisible giant pudding.

Now the members of our cinema-reviewing club are probably more polite than the average teenage person, and even Feet Corbishly, the daughter of ex-flea-hairs, was pretty respectful to adults. But when Professor Purzelbaum's dented orange Gremlin scraped a chestnut tree while making the turn from Varsity Avenue onto Bristle Street, she could not hold her tongue.

"Excuse me, Professor."

"Call me Rafferty."

"Excuse me, Professor Rafferty, but I just wanted to know whether you have had much experience driving, for instance in this city."

She then ducked her head below the level of the window she was sitting beside, because branches were sweeping in and by it.

"Are you criticizing my handling of this vehicle?" asked the Professor, taking his eye off the road. That didn't seem to make any difference.

"Well, yes," said Feet, popping her head up again, and pointing at the pedestrian in the crosswalk.

"Because if you are criticizing my driving, let me point out that I am a man of science, and I know all the mechanical and physical laws pertaining to the movement of this vehicle along its trajectory."

"Trajectory?" yelped Harry.

"Yes but...," said Feet.

"And even though you are unwisely wearing sandals, I have made no critical remarks about your pedal extremities."

All four of us kids sat up straight and started to point out the illogic of that comparison, but before we could say anything much someone else was yelling at us all. This was a middle-aged man in aviator glasses who was hanging onto the hood of the Gremlin and begging the driver to stop.

Professor Purzelbaum pulled over and parked in a driveway between two flat-top apartment buildings.

"Thank you," said the man in the aviator glasses.

"Sorry about that," said Viv, who had jumped out and was now brushing car-dirt off the man's jacket.

"I ought to sue you, said the man. He did not know that he was looking at the side of Professor Purzelbaum's head, because the Professor's eyeglasses had got pushed around ninety degrees.

Eventually we kids placated the man, and he walked off yelling single words.

"Idiot. Law. Knuckles. Jacket. Gremlin. Manslaughter."

"Can I drive?" asked Harry, turning his welder's cap right-side-out.

"You haven't got a license, Harry," I said. "You've never driven a car."

"Can I drive?" asked Harry again.

No such luck. We got into the orange Gremlin, and if you don't know what that looks like, it would be a good idea to look hard for one, or find some old advertisements, or ask your uncle, the one who knows about cars. Because you won't see many of them around.

We were driving through North Ganymede, looking for Fogswept Boulevard. We figured that Professor Purzelbaum ought to meet some real parents. No, that wasn't the right word. Some real extra parents. Some unwanted dads and moms from outer space. Parents from space.

Harry had got over the worst part of his terror, though we all flinched every time the Gremlin passed right by a stop sign. He was sitting up front in the death seat, as they call it.

"Hey, Rochester," he said.

"Yes?" said Professor Purzelbaum.

Viv's eyes shot upward and her hands went like talons into her tangly red hair.

"I was wondering, Prof. I mean let me get back to the question we were considering before. Do you think this could all be a movie we're just actors in?"

"Characters," I put in.

Professor Purzelbaum stopped the car in the middle of the street. Luckily there was not a lot of traffic in this part of North Ganymede.

"Have a good look at me," said the Professor. "Do I look like a movie star? If they were making a movie, would they pick a guy that looks like me to be the central figure?"

"Maybe if it was a teenage horror film," whispered Feet.

I put a knuckle in her ear.

"Are you the central character?" asked Viv.

"You're the movie critic," said the Professor. "Now where is Foot's house?"

"Feet," said Foot, I mean Feet.

"It's right there, across the street," I said.

There was the yellowish-brown VW bus with the flower decals, but the black Mercedes was gone. We couldn't see any faces at any of the windows, upstairs or downstairs. We scanned the imported bushes for skulking relatives. No one.

Professor Purzelbaum let the clutch out and the orange Gremlin jumped a little forward and shivered to a stop, with a loud *auspuff*. We were glad to have our seatbelts on, even if they looked as if they would snap under a moderate karate chop. Viv leaned forward from the back seat and took the key out of the ignition and handed it to the Professor.

"Now what do we do, Herr Prof? asked Harry. I think he was quoting from a movie, but you could never tell for sure with Harry. I mean if he was quoting from a movie, you could never be sure he got it close to right. Once he said to me, "Frankly Charlie, I don't give a hoot."

"We sit tight and wait," said Professor Purzelbaum. "And call me Roderigo."

While we were waiting, and while we were waiting to find out what we were waiting for, we told Professor Purzelbaum about our meeting with Mr Dropo, or rather the Earth-visitor who resembled Mr Dropo. We emphasized his remark that the visitors were ideas.

"They don't drink alcohol, eh?" mused the astronomer.

"They don't smoke, either," said Viv.

"Makes you wonder why we don't want them as visitors, doesn't it?" suggested Prof P.

We all sat and wondered about that for a while. If you have seen a Gremlin you will know that the people in the back seat don't really have windows, so the girls and I were not as lucky as the people in the front. I mean there was a smell of burnt gasoline or whatever fuel that car ran on. It was like the smell around the loading platforms at the bus station. There were other smells, too, but that was the worst one. The front windows were wide open but still we wished we were outside.

But the idea was to remain unnoticed if possible, so we sat tight. Right, five people sitting in a dented orange Gremlin on a street of BMWs and Jaguars. And the guy in the driver's seat has blondish-brown hair hanging from the point of a sugarloaf.

"I wish it was the last ten minutes of a socially significant movie," I said.

"I wish it was the seventh-inning stretch," said the creature from the university.

"Gee, Professor Rosario," you don't seem like the kind of person who would go to the ball game," said Viv.

"That's exactly the kind of person I am. Or I'm exactly and precisely the sort of person who goes to ball games. I used to play longstop for the Renfrew Legion Little League team."

"That's shortstop," I said.

"Whatever."

"It's true," said Harry. "Look around next time you're at the stadium. There's a lot of strange people go to the ball game. Present company excepted, of course."

"What name do you go by in the phone book?" asked Viv.

"Ho ho ho ho," replied the Professor.

"What are we doing sitting here?" asked Feet.

"I have to go to the bathroom," said Harry.

I reached forward and grabbed his shoulders.

"See?" I said. "That proves we aren't in a movie. No one ever says they have to go to the bathroom in a movie."

We all sat in silence for a while, five quiet people in a funny orange car on a quiet winding street in North Ganymede in the shade of a huge chestnut tree on a late afternoon in July. Chickadees squeaked angrily at each other. Once in a while a crow cracked its voice above us somewhere. Two old women in mauve velour jogging suits came running by. They didn't appear to notice us, as if they saw dented orange Gremlins all the time.

Once in a while Harry would grind his teeth and uncross his legs and cross them again the other way, which is not easy even for a short boy who is not in the front seat of that kind of car.

"Hey, Harry," said Feet. "There is half an acre of bushes back of our house. You can go there. My father does before he comes in the house sometimes when he gets home late from one of his Late Evening Board Meetings."

"Naw, I couldn't," said Harry.

"Sure you can. You're not a character from a Major Motion Picture," said Viv.

That was enough to persuade Harry. He got out of the car, stopped to close the door carefully with both hands, and then ran across the street like a kid brother chasing an ice cream vendor. He disappeared around behind the house.

We waited. The highest number of people likely to know what we were waiting for was one.

Harry came tearing back around the house and across the street. He had his hands in front of him, like a sleepwalker doing the hundred meter dash. When he got to the car he grabbed Professor Purzelbaum's door and tried to pull it off the car. He was panting. His welder's cap was nowhere in sight.

"What is it?" asked the Prof.

"What?"

"What, Harry?"

"I beg your pardon?"

Harry panted and panted, his fingers grabbing the door by the window frame. His eyes were wild. He looked like the main actor's kid brother in *Attack of the Giant Gall Bladder*.

"I saw—" he started.

"What?"

"What?"

Etcetera.

"I don't know what I saw. It looked like Feet's father."

"What was he doing in the bushes?" asked Feet.

"Lying there," said Harry.

"On the ground?"

The Professor wolf whistled, and we all shut up. He pushed his hair up with his open hand, and we saw his blue eyes behind and above his glasses, which were almost falling off.

"Harry, I want you to be calm and stop trying to tell us

what you saw. Just let us all get out of the car, and you can lead us to your discovery."

So we all got out and followed Harry around behind the Corbishlys' huge house. We walked single file, in and out among the bushes that looked like the Kaiser Park Arboretum without the glass roof. Then Harry stopped and pointed. He wanted us all to go ahead of him. Maybe he wanted us to corroborate what he had seen. Maybe he was not that eager to see what he had seen again.

And there he was, behind a bush with purple leaves like coins. Mr Corbishly. Except for two things. He might have been Mr Corbishly and he might have been one of the Corbishlys from outer space. And he wasn't really a Mr Corbishly. He was a kind of deflated Mr Corbishly.

I was going to say that things like this are always hard to describe. But that sounds kind of dumb, given the situation, doesn't it?

He was lying on the ground, face up, if it was a face and if it was a he. It looked like an inflatable life-size doll all empty. But the clothes, a shirt and a pair of white corduroy slacks and white socks and running shoes, were real. Everyone was afraid to touch it or say anything.

Feet just stared at it with no expression on her face. There *was* an expression on the flat person's face, a kind of mixture of anger and surprise.

And the colours were fading. Its face and hair were the right shades but not bright enough. The eyes were light light brown.

"Aha!" shouted Professor Purzelbaum. Everyone else jumped. He took out a notebook and began writing in it.

We all waited for whatever was supposed to follow the Aha.

"Did you have an idea, Professor Roseola?" asked Viv at last.

"That *is* an idea," he said, pointing with his pencil.

We were all back in the orange Gremlin, our terror mixed with wonder. The terror was caused by Professor Purzelbaum's driving, which was even worse now, because he was still writing things in his notebook while we were moving. The wonder was caused by our seeing Feet's father fade away. Not really her father—we were sure of that. But one of her fathers from outer space.

How were we supposed to feel?

How, especially, was Feet supposed to feel?

I mean, even though she knew that it was not her dad, it looked like him. It was wearing his clothes. And even if it was a creature from another galaxy, it wasn't a monster.

I mean a father from outer space is not the same thing

as a giant green blob, for instance. You can't call in the air force to fire rockets into a mom or dad from beyond the solar system.

So here was an uninvited house guest, let us say. But he was still a kind of person. When a person shrivels up and fades it isn't the same thing as a balloon losing its air.

"What are we going to do now?" asked Viv.

We were thankful to see Professor Purzelbaum put his notebook away. He started to put his pencil away, too, but it fell down the front of his lab coat and disappeared somewhere, probably under his seat.

"First," he said, "we will make anonymous telephone calls to Louis Boudreau at the *Moon* and Mackenzie MacDonald at the TV station," he said. "Tell them to have a look behind Leg's house."

"Feet," I said.

"Arm," said Harry.

"Then," said Professor Purzelbaum, "we will go to tiffin."

I looked at Viv. Viv looked at Harry. Harry was looking straight ahead at the vacillating road. Feet looked at me, or rather she looked right through my head. None of us wanted to be the first to ask. It was quiet in the Gremlin for a while, if you can call it quiet in a car that sounds as if it is slowly exploding, especially when the driver forgets to use the clutch while changing gears. We were all waiting for someone else to ask.

I noticed that Harry was wearing a dusty Greek fisherman's cap. I still have no idea where he got it.

As we drove down Bristle Street I saw a man on the sun deck of his condo, picking up a dress.

"Tiffin," said Professor Purzelbaum, "is a kind of indoor picnic the British people have in the late afternoon. Like so many British things that one can actually enjoy, it was imported from India."

I guess he had assumed that one of us would break down and ask sooner or later.

"They eat little sandwiches with the crusts cut off the bread and unimaginable things inside. They eat scones with grape jelly. They have dainty savouries. The purists have curry this and that."

"What are dainty savouries?" asked Harry before he could stop himself.

"I don't know," said Professor Purzelbaum.

The noisy silence went on again for a time. While we were mercifully stopped for a red light on Rain Street I looked into a video shop window and saw someone renting a copy of *The Left-Handed Gun*.

Or something anyway. Maybe a western, at least.

"I picked up the habit of tiffin," said Professor Purzelbaum, "while I was enjoying an exchange scholarship in the scenic little city of Preston, Lancashire, home of the British wood duck."

"So where are we going for this tiffing?" asked Viv.

"No no, dear, tiffin. It is not a present participle. Eating is a present participle. Tiffing would mean squabbling over your food or something. Our little English repast is called tiffin. No *g*."

Viv's eyes rolled around 720 degrees. She is the best eye-roller in Major Douglas High School.

"Okay, Doctor, where do you plan to do this tiffin'?" she asked.

"Hmm."

"Hmmm?"

"No, hmm. I think I'll hold out for the Food Fair."

He stuck his left arm straight out the window and yanked the steering wheel to the right. Car horns demonstrated the Doppler effect and certain robust male voices reached us through the sudden traffic noise. The Gremlin was going down some dark ramp and then we were stopped. We all had to get out on the driver's side because the other side was four centimeters from a concrete wall.

"One of these doors takes us to the Downtown Twelve Food Fair," said Professor Purzelbaum, and strode toward a door with some kind of numbers painted on it. A pencil rolled on the grey painted concrete floor behind him.

We all followed.

After visits to various steam rooms and storage closets, we found our way to the Food Fair. I remember the one time my sister and I came here with my parents. It was one of those times when someone decided that the family should try to do things together. We had been to see a movie. I didn't tell my parents that I had already seen it and reviewed it. It was *Rotting Teenagers II*. Anyway, when we came down to the Food Fair for a snack afterward, my father said "Food Fair? It just looks like a lot of booths offering franchise fast foods. Where are the clowns? Where are the balloons and organ grinder music?"

"I'll organ grinder you if I don't get something to eat fast," my mother said.

So here we were. Harry, of course, was filled with consternation. He hated to make a choice among enchiladas, fish 'n chips and the Great Goopburger. Feet headed straight for the salad bar. Viv was standing and reading the wall menu at Rumanian Roger's, even though there were only three items, and she knew them off by heart. She always wound up with onion rings and a milkshake anyway. I was standing in the Chinese food lineup, already planning on the lemon chicken. Professor Purzelbaum was in front of me.

"I wonder," he said, "whether I might substitute in the combinations."

"Substitute?" asked the middle-aged Chinese woman behind the steam table.

"Mix and match," said Professor Purzelbaum.

"You want combination six? We have no combination six," she said authoritatively.

"No, no. Look, I would like to keep the fried rice from combination three, but instead of the chow mein I would like the egg foo young from combination two and instead of the sweet and sour I would like the snow peas from combination five."

"You want fried rice and egg foo young on the same dish?" asked the woman.

"What's wrong with that?" asked the Prof.

"That's crazy," said the woman. You think we don't know what we're doing when we make up these combinations?"

"Well, no—"

"And put the numbers on them?"

"What about fried rice and chow mein?" asked the Prof. "I would never think of putting them in the same combination."

"What are you, a scientist or an artist?" she asked.

"I'm just a customer right now," said the Prof.

"Do you always have this much trouble in eating places?" she asked. Now she had managed to put on a look that combined sympathy and a bit of distaste.

"May I have some steamed rice and a Diet Slurp," said the Prof.

He didn't look defeated, exactly. Professor Purzelbaum seemed like the kind of person who could eat steamed rice and Diet Slurp for tiffin every day.

I got my lemon chicken and a cup of tea and joined the others at one of the round butcher-block tables surrounded by unmovable round butcher-block stools. They were unbelievably uncomfortable. And there were only four seats. The four of us who were lucky enough to sit on them felt our knees mashed against the sides of the butcher-block table. Harry sat on a seat at the next table and leaned toward us. He was sipping chocolate-blueberry soda water through a straw.

Professor Purzelbaum pushed his hair back off what turned out to be his forehead, straightened his glasses as best he could, and ripped open and emptied four little packettes of soya sauce onto his steamed rice. Then he got up and went back to the Chinese food counter to get a little white plastic fork.

"What are we doing here?" whispered Harry. He had his Greek fisherman's hat on backward.

"Tiffin'," replied Viv, also in a whisper.

I turned to watch Professor Purzelbaum come back, maybe to make sure he found his way. In a corner of the Food Fair I saw a boy sitting at one of the tables with three identical fathers.

That reminded me to get down to business when our scientist got back to us.

"Sir," I said.

"Call me Reynaldo."

Feet sighed audibly. I shot her a look.

"Professor Purzelbaum, Rey, Sir," I said. "What are we going to do about the problem of the parents from outer space?"

"*Perhaps* from outer space."

"Perhaps, sir, from outer space. Or let me put it this way. Where do we stand now? What is your opinion on this matter?"

He put a huge clump of dark brown rice into the front side of his head. Then he looked at me, or so it seemed, while he chewed a little and swallowed a lot.

"I subscribe to your theory that these creatures are ideas," he said.

"So you agree with the psychology professor?"

"No, I do not. He believes that they are *your* ideas. I think they are *their* ideas."

He went to sit back, but there are no backs to the butcher-block seats. Viv and Feet grabbed him in time. It would have been awfully embarrassing to have to pick him up off the floor. A pencil fell out of his lab coat and flipped end over end and settled against another table block.

I thought about his distinction regarding whose ideas these strange folk were. I was glad to hear that he didn't think we were seeing things. On the other hand, how much were we supposed to be encouraged by support from a grownup like that? I mean look at the way he drives, and look what he eats.

Still, I would rather agree with Professor Rosario Purzelbaum than with Doctor Hosenklappe, the psychology professor.

I waited for the Professor to finish his dark wet rice. I spent most of that time looking elsewhere. The table full of dads seemed awfully quiet. I tried to think of them as ideas, but that isn't easy. It is probably easier to see something that is not there than to see something that is there and have to tell yourself that it is only sort of there.

At last Professor Purzelbaum located the last little grain of rice on his styrofoam plate and got it into his mouth. We had all finished our varied eats some time before, except for Harry, who had gone back for a hotdog. I could not bear to watch him, either. Like a lot of poor uninformed kids lately, he had ketchup on his hotdog. No mustard, no relish, no onions, just ketchup. He also puts ketchup on his hamburgers. He is my friend, but sometimes I don't know why.

"Well," said Viv, slapping her hands together, and interlacing her fingers, "now what are we going to do?"

"Go home for supper," said Professor Purzelbaum.

"What?" said Viv.

"Okay, dinner. Whatever you call it at your house."

"We came down here to do some tiffin', and now we just go home and forget all about our problems?"

"No, for three of you your problems are at home," he said, and his glasses fell off and bounced on the table.

Harry handed them over to him.

"Perhaps also the beginnings of your solutions. I think it is a good idea to keep your eyes open. Make a note of anything that might appear useful," said the Professor.

"When shall we five meet again?" asked Feet.

A big grin appeared under the hair on the Professor's face.

"Ah, the mortal bard," he proclaimed.

"Huh?" put in Harry.

"Tonight we will all escape our various domiciles by whatever means necessary," said our scientist. "Then we will go and pay a visit to one Mr Dropo. We will convene at eleven p.m. in the Blam Cafe on Kaiser Street. They have terrific applesauce cake."

"Aha," I suggested. "I think I am beginning to see the outlines of the plan."

"Just one Mr Dropo," said the Prof.

I wish I could tell you what went on over the supper hour in Feet's house, and Viv's house, and Harry's big old apartment over on Watercress Crescent. But for that you would need a different kind of narrator. Maybe a storyteller from outer space.

When I got home my mother was sitting in the kitchen, her purse on the kitchen table, a very long cigarette held to her lips.

"Glad to see you could find time to make us a visit," she said. Her words were made of blue-grey smoke. She breathed in another sentence from the burning leaf-fragments.

My grandmother was sitting in the livingroom, watching a cartoon about a cat that could move only one part of his body at a time.

"You young gangsters have been out putting coppers and nails on the train tracks again, haven't you?" she enquired.

My sister zipped through the room and headed for the staircase.

"It's your turn to take out the compost bucket, Mucus Face," she said over her shoulder.

My father was on the front porch, sitting on a white plastic chair and reading the new issue of *Lonesome Whistle*.

"Hi, Dad," I said.

"Well, hmmpff nnnuh yeah, uh huh," he said.

"You are my one and only father," I said. "And I can't tell you how glad I am about that."

He put down his magazine and looked up at me over the tops of his glasses. I always like it when he does that. He looked sort of the way I imagine he used to look when he was a young newspaper guy.

"Well, hmmmpff, I must say, I am glad to hear that, Neville."

"In fact," I went on, "I am glad to have just this one family. One of everything."

"Ah, you're talking about these stories of ghost parents."

"Well, actually, even if I wasn't I would still be glad you're my only folks," I said.

"Did you see the headline on page three of the *Moon*?"

The paper was neatly folded and lying on the white plastic table. I opened it neatly.

TALES OF EXTRANEOUS RELATIVES PERSIST, the headline muttered.

"They really need you down there, Dad," I said, smiling like a dutiful pal of a son.

"Sometimes I think of cutting my vacation short, I must admit," he said, with a dad smile.

I folded the paper carefully and put it down on the

table. My father reached out and shifted it just a little, so that it was lying just the way it had been.

"Dad, I am going to sneak out of the house tonight about ten-thirty, in case you hear a noise."

"Okay, Son," he said.

I was kind of full of Food Fair food. It wasn't funny how full I felt for the first time that day. But free food never fails to fill me with fearful furious appetite. So when supper came (we never called it dinner at our place unless there were guests) I thought I would manage to eat in my normal healthy teenage fashion.

But I did have that glop in my stomach. No, that wasn't it. I was all excited and maybe a little bit scared about what was going to happen after eleven p.m. Well, that might have been it a little bit. But supper was reheated leg of lamb and beets and store-bought potato salad. That's what did it.

"Where's your appetite, young man?" asked my grandmother. "Did you have a big bottle of Kik Cola before supper again?"

"Mum, they haven't been making Kik Cola for thirty years," said my mother.

"Except in Quebec," said my father.

"I had a glass of Kik Cola just the other day," said my grandmother.

My sister was beginning to put on her teenager face. You know, the pretended boredom, the impatience with everything unteenage in the world.

"Where did you come from, Granny?" she asked, "Some other planet?"

We all stopped eating and stared at her, except for my grandmother, who was staring at the beet juice on her sleeve.

"What's the matter? What did I say?" asked Roseanne.

We told her.

She said this was the first she had heard about extra parents from outside the galaxy. She said she hadn't read about it, which I believed, because she never read anything. She said she hadn't heard about it because the only thing she had watched on television was rock videos. I believed her. I guess she didn't pay more than the usual sisterly attention when the four of us were explaining things in the kitchen.

But that made me nervous. I mean there must be other people like her, probably lots of them, teenagers who don't read anything, grownups who watch game shows on television. I once heard of some high school teachers who went to the pub after school on Friday afternoon instead of heading for the library.

"I had a glass of Kik Cola just yesterday," said my grandmother.

Other than that, no one said anything till it was time for dessert. Dessert was orange jello and sliced bananas going brown. I gobbled mine up.

"A sudden return of appetite," observed my father.

I grinned at him and then wiped the grin off when my mother looked at me. Why not? They are both my parents, the only ones I have.

"Can we discuss this problem?" I asked.

"Children are to be seen and not heard," said my grandmother.

"The only problem around here is you," said Ronnie.

She had piled her banana slices in a little tower on the table beside her dish.

"Well it doesn't appear to be *our* problem, does it?" remarked my mother.

"That depends," put in my father, "on your definition of the first person plural. It can be seen as an ethical rather than a proprietory question, certainly."

"That's what I say," I said.

"Well, I don't know about you, but I have things to do," said my sister, standing up and scraping her chair back on the kitchen floor.

"Just don't tie the phone up all night," said my mother, finding a little space to grind out her cigarette among the other cigarettes in her ashtray. She got up, taking her plate and the beet bowl with her.

My grandmother was asleep in her chair. She looked like a very nice lady. I was glad to have her as a grandmother.

My father wiped imaginary crumbs off his shirt front. He shifted his chair back a little so that he could cross his legs. He reached into his shirt pocket and took out his ivory toothpick and started probing for bits of food between his teeth. My mother said it was a brutish habit, but the dentist said it was a good idea.

I shifted my chair back and crossed my legs. I took a sip out of my glass of milk. It was just a little sour.

"So what's your theory?" asked my father.

"How do you know I have a theory?" I asked, without innocence.

"I know you, Neville. You could not go this far without a theory."

"You're right."

"So?"

"I think they are ideas," I said.

"The Creatures?"

"Ideas of some sort. That's what I haven't got figured out. Professor Purzelbaum agrees with me."

My father had succeeded in yanking a little shred of sheep meat out of a crevice somewhere in the rear portion of his mouth. He sucked on his teeth experimentally.

"Ideas, eh?"

"That's my idea."

"Don't make it too complicated," he said with a smile.

"We have visitors from outer space and you want it to be simple?"

"Good point. So what about your idea about these ideas?"

"I haven't got much further than that," I admitted.

"But tonight you expect to find out more," he said.

"Somebody has to," I said.

"Why don't you leave it to the police?" he suggested.

There is always someone who has to say that. At least in American movies and novels. That's because in the United States you are supposed to be west of the law. You are supposed to do what organized law enforcement, as they say, can't do.

"Ah, you know the answer to that, Dad. The police still haven't got around to believing the kids who tell them about their extra parents."

"Can you blame them?" asked my father, who had made a lot of headlines about the police.

"Well, it seems to me that the police should have more experience with weird people, including weird parents, than anyone else," I suggested.

"You have a point there," said my father, with a rhythm in his voice that announced the end of that enquiry.

The television set was howling in the livingroom at ten-thirty, so I made my way easily out the back door. I haven't got a key to our house, so I did what I always do—I stuck my student's card between the lock and the lock-hole. I always figured that I was more likely to use it than a burglar was, and if a burglar did beat me there, what would he get? He couldn't take the television set because someone would probably be watching it.

Off I headed to the Blam Cafe, on foot. I thought that if I walked briskly I could make it there in lots of time, and on the way I would be stimulating my brain to turn over the things I knew so far and to try to peek under the corners of the things I didn't know.

In my life I have spent a lot of time playing private detective. I have even followed someone all day just for practice. Just for practice at first, and then because it gets interesting. You might think that most people you see walking by are living pretty dull lives. But if you start following someone all day, adding bits of information as you go along, you will see that there probably isn't such a thing as a dull life. I mean outside the family, anyway. Some day get me to tell you about the time I followed the woman who left a whole outfit of new-looking clothes in a telephone booth in front of the Culpepper Hotel.

I was walking good and fast. On occasions such as this I usually carry on a conversation in my head. I will bet that a lot of people do that. Maybe everyone does. Maybe my mother does.

Sometimes, if there isn't anyone else around, or if I am out at night walking across a park, I will carry on these conversations out loud, in a kind of whisper, something halfway between a whisper and quiet regular talking.

"All right," I said, my breath worked up by the quick walking. "That deflated doll-human being behind Feet's house has to be the skin of one of these alien parents. The question is: do they shed their skin the way snakes do, or does a skin mean a defunct parent?"

I listened to myself saying this, all the time switching my eyes back and forth, looking for something behind every tree. There were quite a few regular people on the street, at least regular for people around Kaiser Park and Kannegeiser Beach.

"Sure, that's *one* of the questions," I replied, also in a kind of whisper-talk. "But here's another one: if they shed their skin, why do they do that? Is it because they want to change identity, to become someone else's parent? Or do they have to make a new skin every day or so?"

"Snakes don't do it every day," I said.

"Snakes don't come from outer space," I rejoined. "Now here is another question, still dealing with your one question."

"I was kind of looking for answers when I put out my question," I said, a little impatiently.

"That isn't the way life works. That is the way school works. In life when you ask a question you usually get back another question. Sometimes questions are the best answers."

"Oh great, now I'm dealing with a philosopher! Being a film critic isn't enough for you. Now you have to be a philosopher."

I tried to give myself a look of impatience, but I couldn't move fast enough. I was reminded of the time I told Harry I had managed to bite myself on the forehead by standing on a chair. He believed me for about ten minutes. I couldn't get over it. So anyway, I let a little impatience creep into my voice.

"Anyway. If you discover a skin because an alien parent is a goner, the question is: what finished him or her off?"

"There are, of course, the following moral questions. Such as: how do we respond to that? Do we find out what finished the parent from space and use it to finish or drive off the rest of them? Or is patricide still a crime if it is a newly-minted father we are despatching?"

"Aha! Now who's the philosopher?" I asked.

I smiled ruefully at a dark tree because I couldn't depend on my seeing it. I was through Kaiser Park and walking quickly up Kaiser Street. I didn't even stop to look at a guy who was using a spraypaint can to write a sentence on the side of the Smedley Theatre.

What he had finished so far was: WHAT IS WORSE, IGNORANCE OR A

I was, meanwhile, carrying on the conversation with myself. I had left morality and big words aside, and was now onto the subject that must be bothering you as much as it bothered me.

"What I would like to know, and I suppose what we would all like to know, is: why isn't there a great city-wide panic about this invasion?"

"Invasion? I don't see any invasion," I replied, probably for the sake of argument. "In an invasion you feel threatened by the aggressive and violent behaviour of the invaders. All these people or creatures are guilty of is wanting to be parents."

"There's another question," I cut in. "Why are they here? I don't mean why are they here instead of on another non-invaded planet. But why are they here instead of back home? How many of them came? Did they abandon their own children? Etcetera, Neville."

"Let's get back to the question of why there isn't a general panic among the populace, as they say. I mean here we are, getting invaded or at least visited from outer space, and you would think it was just a state visit from some little South American country you haven't heard of."

"There isn't any South American country I haven't heard of: Colombia, Venezuela, Ecuador, Surinam, Guyana—"

"All right, all right. But answer me this question: how come the army and air force aren't buzzing around? How come there aren't riots in the streets? Why are people mainly treating this as business as usual?"

"Maybe things would be different if Dad was writing the headlines this week."

"Neville..."

"Maybe Mackenzie MacDonald at the TV station is sitting on the story because he was an orphan

"All right, if you aren't going to be serious..."

"How can you be serious about having four pairs of moms and dads sitting in the livingroom?"

"Okay. But how come the public hasn't gone bonkers? How come this event is a semi-secret?"

I stopped walking for a moment and turned to face me, but I wasn't there. I spoke out loud anyway.

"Do you remember the day of the San Francisco earthquake? Remember it hit just before the third game of the World Series at Candlestick Park? They had to evacuate sixty thousand fans and players and umpires and so on."

"Yeah, it shook the stadium even worse than the Athletics' hitters would have," I said.

"Well, I was watching the news that was on television instead of the ball game. It was an hour after the quake, and they were interviewing the commissioner of baseball on camera, and in the background I could hear some guys shouting 'Come on! PLAY BALL!' "

"I see what you mean," I replied. "But I'm not sure I'm satisfied. In any case, here we are at the Blam Cafe."

"I knew that," I said.

I was the last one there. Except for Professor Purzelbaum.

"We decided that we might as well have a little something while we were waiting," said Harry. He was starting on the second half of a toasted mushroom and tuna sandwich. Harry is always doing that in the Blam Cafe. He has never yet ordered off the menu, which, as I said, mainly consists of triangular sandwiches in plastic wrapping you could challenge a brain surgeon to remove. But they always make what he asks for. He was drinking a coconut whizz with a bunch of maraschino cherries in it.

On his head there was a plastic yellow imitation hard hat that bore the word TONKA.

The girls were not having anything. When Harry said

they were having a little something, he was using the editorial "we" we had been hearing about in English class.

"Have you heard from the Professor?" I asked.

Harry thought it was better for him to talk with his mouth full of toast and tuna and mushrooms, than for one of the girls to answer.

"Hmfgh guppig imminug, whald due fron ga—"

"What your friend Mr Fieldstone is saying, in the language he perhaps picked up from a stray parent, is that there was a telephone message for us from the Professor," said Feet, with a look that said she was only barely hanging on to some resolve to indulge her friend in the hat.

"Said he came early and sat there for a half an hour before he noticed he was sitting in the Wham Sandwich Bar instead of the Blam Cafe," explained Viv. Her eyes were dancing.

This is wonderful. What am I doing here? I asked myself. Here we were laying our lives in the hands of a scientist who is supposed to know his way around the almost limitless universe, but who has trouble figuring out where he is on Kaiser Street.

Then I saw a white lab coat out of the corner of my eye.

"There he is now," said Feet, who did not change her facial expression for the new subject of her sentence.

Professor Purzelbaum would have walked right past our table, but Viv reached out and got a handful of his lab coat as he was passing. He pushed his glasses up his nose, where they rested crookedly for a moment before falling back down. I could see a blue eye between stalks of falling hay.

"Aha, there you are!" he exclaimed.

A waitress arrived wearing the name Patti on a badge.

"A pot of tea and five orders of raisin toast, please," said the Professor, pulling over a chair from the next table.

"Applesauce cake," said Viv.

"And applesauce cake," instructed the Professor.

Patti smiled and scooted off to the kitchen hole, casting four quick glances at the newcomer. She probably thought there was an invasion of some sort of hay people from outer space.

"What's the plan, Reynaldo?" asked Feet.

The Professor looked left and right, quickly. We all followed suit. I looked across the cafe. Patti looked left and right. The cook's head came through the kitchen hole. He looked left and right.

Then we all fixed our gaze on the Professor.

"Tonight at midnight, Mr Dropo will depart the Thunderdog Neighbourhood Pub. There we will—"

He stopped abruptly as Patti placed the big brown teapot and five cups and saucers and spoons on the table in front of us.

"There you go!" she said with fervour.

Harry handed her his used dish and glass. Then we all waited in silence for the rest of Professor Purzelbaum's sentence. When he said "we" he meant all five of us.

Professor Purzelbaum didn't start talking again.

"There we will—?" whispered Feet.

"Aha!" said Professor P. "There we will intercept him. This will be the Mr Dropo you spoke with before, the one who has discovered the human consumption of imbibable alcohol. There we will intercept him, take him somewhere, perhaps some coffee shop you might know of."

"Flics," said Harry.

"No, no, a cafe. We wouldn't find a movie theatre open at that time of night."

"Flics is the name of our favourite cappuccino bar," said Viv.

"Flics it is, then," said the Professor. "There we will sober our friend up to a certain extent with strong Italian coffee."

"Ukrainian-Italian java," said Harry.

"There you *go!*" said Patti. She laid the raisin toast and jam jars and applesauce cake and forks and knives down in front of us.

We used the few moments of silence to stick jam on our toast. I grabbed the ginger marmalade before Harry could get it.

"And then—?" asked Feet.

"Then? Oh, then. Then," said Professor P, "we shall interrogate him. The key to coping with an interstellar visit or invasion, depending on your point of view, is to learn as much as possible about your visitor or invader, depending on your point of view again."

We ate up all the toast and applesauce cake, and drank most of the tea, except for Harry, who wouldn't touch his after an exploratory sip. Then the Professor tried to pay for all of it but couldn't find his wallet. I took care of the bill, and out we went.

Professor Purzelbaum's car was standing ready for use in front of the Smedley Theatre. We persuaded him that it was just a short walk, and that it was really hard to find a parking space near the Thunderdog Neighbourhood Pub.

I saw the finished spraybomb writing on the side of the Smedley Theatre. It said: WHAT IS WORSE, IGNORANCE OR APATHY?

Underneath, in the same handwriting: I DON'T KNOW AND I DON'T CARE.

It was a bit of a walk, and Harry could be heard making himself huff and puff, hoping for pity or mercy or at least sympathy. Professor Purzelbaum had a mysterious or secret look on his face. I wondered whether the others noticed. It should have been a dark night overhead because there was an unseen thick layer of clouds between us and the stars. But the lights of the city seemed to bounce back down off that ceiling. What light there was, however, was converted in our minds, or in mine anyway, into something spooky. The night of the living bed. Something as scary as that.

We arrived at a bus shelter across the street from the Thunderdog Neighbourhood Pub. Harry sat down on the bench. The rest of us gathered around the Prof.

"How do you know Mr Dropo's in there?" asked Viv.

"I don't think Mr Dropo is in there," said Prof Purzelbaum, who seemed to be enjoying this investigative procedure. "I think his clone is."

"Clone?"

"Or rather his probably extraterrestrial duplicate."

Two men and two women came out the front door of the Thunderdog. They were talking loudly, all four at once, and walking unsteadily. It appeared that they thought each other to be the best company in the world. They knocked into one another as they proceeded to the little parking lot beside the pub. I guess they weren't from the neighbourhood. I did a little hope inside my head that they would get where they were going without hitting anyone nice.

"Okay, Doctor Raffaeli P," said Feet. "How do you know that our target will be coming out of that place at midnight?"

Professor Purzelbaum pushed his hair aside so we could see the satisfied smile all over his face, his straw-coloured eyebrows pushed up high.

"Research!" he said.

I haven't told my colleagues, but it was at this point that I began to think of Professor Purzelbaum as a role model. While I was home having an unmemorable meal with my immediate family, thank goodness, he was doing research. It was soon after this that I vowed to practice time management the rest of my life. Except on those rare occasions when the Winnipeg Jets are playing on television.

More people were coming out of the pub. Some of them were laughing. It was not a rainy night, so no one was in a hurry. One of them started to fall down, but saved himself by grabbing the front of his friend's coat and almost pulling him down. This didn't really look like a lot of fun, but who am I to judge? A young woman's loud laughter sounded like the call of a loon across a narrow lake.

"There he is," said Viv.

"There *they* are," amended Feet.

Mr Dropo came walking down the four steps outside the pub door, his arm around Mr Dropo's shoulders. They were singing, or trying to sing, a song that has never been in the Top Forty. When they reached the paved surface of the ground, they started to walk in opposite directions. Then they turned and walked toward each other and in fact bumped into each other.

I remembered what Mr Dropo had told us about the novelty of alcohol as something to pour down your throat.

"Now what?" whispered Viv.

Now what indeed. Now one of the Mr Dropos did something none of us expected. He did something none of us would have thought it was possible for him to do. I mean even if he had not been in the Thunderdog Neighbourhood Pub all evening, he would have amazed us by doing what he did.

This Mr Dropo flipped himself upside down and started walking on his hands toward the sidewalk that bordered Bristle Street.

"Holy cow!" was Harry's opinion.

But that was nothing compared to what the other Mr Dropo did. The other Mr Dropo took a look at the first Mr Dropo walking on his hands, then proceeded to top that stunt with one of his own.

His eyes opened wide. We could see the street lights reflecting off them from across the street. Then all the air came out of him in a whoosh, and he flew like a released balloon, in mad loops and unfinished circles. We watched in amazement and the beginning of horror. In what seems like an hour on remembering, but in what must have been a few seconds, this Mr Dropo's empty skin and clothes lay limp over the hood of a 1988 Honda Civic.

The other Mr Dropo was on his feet again, and he just barely beat us to the skin and clothes. Only then did we notice that there had been someone inside the car. She got out and looked unhappily on the phenomenon. She had been in the pub for a while, it appeared.

"Oh great!" she said. "I suppose my insurance isn't going to cover this."

"It doesn't look as if there is any damage to your car," said Professor Purzelbaum.

"Oh yeah?" she shouted. "Oh yeah? Look at that dent."

The dent was in the rear left fender. It was all rusty.

"It looks as if that has been there for approximately twelve months," said Prof. P.

"Oh yeah? Well, how am I going to get home with that thing on the front of my car?" she demanded.

There was a small crowd now, most of it made up of people who said things that didn't make much sense to anyone who had been around the Thunderdog for just a few minutes. Viv went to the pub to ask someone to call the authorities. There wasn't a policeman within shouting distance. They don't like to look as if they are interfering when a lot of drunk people are getting into their automobiles.

A young man reached out to touch the deflated alien. The remaining Mr Dropo grabbed his arm and pulled him away.

"Don't you touch my buddy," he said.

"Buddy?" said a voice from the crowd. "The poor sap. Has to have a blow-up doll for a drinking buddy."

"Yeah, come on, let's get to the Brambledairy, I mean Brambergarry, ah, what's the place...?"

"The Brambleberry Arms," said his chum.

"Yeah, the Gramblebamble Arms. It don't close till one-thirty."

A number of cars could be heard noisily and inefficiently leaving the parking lot. Despite our attempts to stop her, the woman with the 1988 Honda Civic got back into her car and backed away. The deflated Mr Dropo fell off and landed on its flat face.

Now there were only the six of us waiting for the police.

"Excuse me," said Professor Purzelbaum to the remaining Mr Dropo. "Are you from another galaxy?"

This Mr Dropo was a little the worse for wear all at once. He leaned against the side of the Thunderdog Pub. He burped.

"Heck no," he said at last, in that loud rasping voice you associate with people who spend a lot of time smoking cigarettes in beer parlours. "I'm from Saskabush, Saskatchewan. Came out here twenty-twelve years ago. Never had any brothers or sisters, till just recently. Never saw anyone turn into a balloon before, either. Never used to have people doing that in Saskatchewan. The Keystone Province."

"Home of the Big Green Machine," said Harry.

"A Massey Ferguson combine?" asked Viv.

"The Saskatchewan Roughriders," said Harry, scornfully.

I thought it was a pretty dumb time to be discussing football. Even Professor Purzelbaum looked a little impatient.

A police car arrived with lights flashing around but no siren. Two policemen with about twenty heavy objects hanging off their belts got out. As they were approaching, Mr Purzelbaum spoke quickly to the remaining Mr Dropo.

"After we are finished with the police, I want to ask you for a favour," he said.

"Oh sure, anything," said Mr Dropo. He sounded a little sarcastic.

"How many more of you are there at home?"

"Just two," said Mr Dropo.

"I would like to meet one of them," said Professor Purzelbaum. "Here."

Well, I took the gang, except for Professor Purzelbaum, over to my house for camping out again. It was one thing to go home for supper with the expanded family, I suppose. I couldn't really know what it must be like to be surrounded by fake parents. But they let me know, all three of them, that they didn't like the idea of sleeping overnight in a house full of aliens.

As far as we knew, the visitors did not have any evil intent planned, nothing worse than what you might expect from normal parents, that is. They hadn't zapped anyone with a ray gun or melted anyone with cybernetic brainwaves, all that stuff we knew from science horror movies. My favourite was *Attack of the Giant Leeches*. It contains the immortal line spoken by one of the female victims: "Oh no, not again!"

There are science fiction stories, though, that tell you

about seemingly friendly space creatures that destroy the earth accidentally, or that start off being friendly and get you off your guard and then start eating you or something like that. If you let down your guard and then later lost your left leg to a hungry Martian, there would be no going back.

Anyway, I figured that my mother and sister and grandmother were not going to get much more annoyed than they already were, so I invited my group over to flop at the old homestead again. I knew I didn't have to worry about my father. He thinks everything is interesting. That is what makes him a good headline writer.

Before we went to our various beds and couches and sleeping bags we sat at the kitchen table and had a late late night snack. Three of us had chocolate milk and vegetable snaps, little triangular crackers. Harry ate most of a head of raw cauliflower, and drank some cold beef bouillon.

It had been a pretty exciting night, and the police had held on to us till two in the morning. Now it was nearly three, but we were so excited that it was going to be hard for most of us to get to sleep. Harry was snoring in five minutes.

Viv eventually fell asleep with her head on her arms on the table. Feet and I picked her up and put her on the couch in the livingroom with a blanket over her. Then we found our usual sleeping places and crashed for what turned out to be about three and a half hours.

I woke up to a peculiar noise I could not identify. It sounded a little like a squirrel I once heard screaming because it had its leg caught in the screen door of the house across the street.

I saw Harry's head emerge from the pile of coats and other clothes on the floor beside my bed.

"What's that?" he enquired. "It sounds like a chain saw trying to go through a really hard knot in a jack pine tree."

I got out of my bed the usual way, headfirst on the floor, then hands on the floor, then whole body on the floor, then upright. I felt around and was assured that my head was still on my neck with the face forward. Good. I passed from my room into the hall and headed for the front door. Viv was arriving there just before me. Her red hair was sticking out in every direction except straight back, and she was holding a blanket around her shoulders.

"It sounds as if someone is pulling boards off the side of a house," she said.

Feet's voice came like the voice of a troll from the livingroom.

"Is there an elephant dying on the front lawn?" she asked.

I opened the door a crack. Then I opened it wider, and three of us looked out. It was the orange Gremlin. Professor Purzelbaum was honking the horn. I looked at my watch. It was eight in the morning.

Then I looked at my father's face at the top of the stairs.

"Tell your friends with the rock and roll saxophone that it is early in the morning on Bicuspid Avenue. Your mother desires a little tranquillity," he informed us, then disappeared into their room.

"I'll tranquillity her," I said under my breath.

"Neville! Tch!" admonished Viv.

Professor Purzelbaum was out of his car and approaching the house. At least it looked as if that was what he was doing. The way he walks it is not easy to see right away what he is up to.

"Thanks for opening the door," he shouted. "I didn't know which house you live in, so I honked the horn."

"So you are the elephant," said Feet, who was now at the door with us.

She had her sandals on and was holding a sleeping bag around her body. Her hair was not mussed at all.

"What?" asked Professor Purzelbaum.

"Elephant," said Harry.

"Private joke," said Viv.

"I stumbled over something after leaving you last night," said the Professor, and as he did his foot hit a little raised part of our front walk and he nearly pitched forward onto his face.

"Was that just last night?" asked Feet with a grimace. "It seems like a week ago."

"Come on, you lot. I'll buy breakfast," said the Professor.

"You lot?"

That was what my mother had called us the day before, I thought.

"It's an English expression I picked up at Oxford."

"During tiffing?" asked Viv.

Breakfast at the Blam Cafe is famous. Everyone within two hundred kilometers knows enough to avoid it.

I had a bowl of corn flakes and milk and a cup of tea. Viv had a bowl of rice crispies and milk and a cup of tea. Feet had a bowl of bran flakes and milk and a cup of hot chocolate because her parents were always drinking tea made of some bushes in the back yard, I mean garden. The Professor was just having coffee and toast.

Harry Fieldstone had pancakes and imitation maple syrup, two fried eggs sunny side up, sausages with HP sauce on them, half a grapefruit with a maraschino cherry in the middle, a bottle of pineapple-raspberry cordial, and a chocolate-vanilla creme doughnut.

"What did you stumble on, Roderigo?" asked Feet.

Professor Purzelbaum calmly began spreading peanut butter on his toast, a combination I have never been able to understand.

"I have begun to formulate a theory," he replied.

"Have you offered it to the police?" asked Harry.

Harry had left his Tonka hard hat somewhere and had somehow managed to get his hands on, and his head into, a yellow plastic Nor'wester rain hat.

"No," said Professor P. "Nor to Mackenzie Mac Donald."

I hated watching Harry eat all that stuff. A whole sausage in his mouth at once, egg yolk all over a pancake. One thing I could never stand is pancakes and syrup and eggs on the same plate. Grease and syrup. Agh, if you will pardon the expression. Harry had various liquids on his chin. I tried not to look.

"Can I have a side order of hashbrowns?" he asked the waitress who was gliding by with a stained coffee pot.

"Can you tell us something about your theory?" I asked the Prof. "Also, can you tell us why we are up so early and sitting in the Blam?"

Professor Purzelbaum took a bite out of the corner of his toast and signified with his eyes that as soon as he had chewed it awhile, he would be able to reply to my questions.

"It just fell into my lap," he said. "Oops."

He had dropped his modified triangle of toast, peanut butter side down, of course, and it missed his plate, missed the table top, and came to a precarious rest on his trousers. He slipped sideways out of his seat, and the toast fell onto the floor, peanut butter side down. Professor Purzelbaum bent to pick it up, and looked as if he were going to brush it off and maybe continue eating it. In the nick of time,

Viv snapped it from his hand and put it on her own plate, peanut butter side down. She put her spoon on top of it. Then she moved her plate as far from the Professor as she could.

He sat down again, and picked up his last half-slice of toast. Three of us watched intently. Harry slurped down the last of his pineapple-raspberry cordial and lifted his hand to signal for something else.

"Your theory, Professor?" I resumed.

"Perhaps it is subjective," he said, popping the rest of his toast into his mouth and signalling that he would be chewing for a while.

We waited.

"Subjective?" asked Viv after a while.

"Mmfggmm ghmmdt prrgh," he said, pointing at his mouth.

"Nnndhd ffmmrmm ghrrkl," said Harry, pushing his plate of multicoloured smears away a little, and chewing something big.

We just had to wait.

While we waited I wondered: why do we seem to spend so much time in cafes?

Now the Professor gulped his last two gulps and began to speak.

"Now, Miss Foot," he said.

"Feet," I said.

"Yes, Miss Feet."

"That's Ms," I said.

"Of course. Ms Feet. Do your parents, or does either of your parents, walk around on his or her hands?"

"I beg your pardon," said Feet. "And don't bother with the Ms."

"I am thinking," said Prof P, "of that first deflated skin we found in your back yard."

"In my neighbourhood you don't say back yard. You say garden," said Feet.

Harry grinned and gave her a little pop punch on the shoulder. She gave him a look that was meant to signify that she could hardly bear to be sitting beside someone so much younger and less mature than herself.

"I get it," I said. "You are putting together the first deflated alien and the second deflated alien."

"That is called the scientific method," said Professor Purzelbaum.

"Aha! That's wonderful!" shouted Viv.

"Not wonderful. Just methodical," said the Prof.

"No," said Feet.

Professor Purzelbaum parted the hair falling over his eyes and poked his bandaged eyeglasses up to the top of his long nose. They fell halfway down again. He sniffed.

"In what way have I fallen short of methodical?" he asked, his back straight and his head held back so he could look at Feet through his glasses.

"No, I have never seen either of my parents walking upside down."

I wanted in on this. I felt that at last we were getting somewhere. I was all for the scientific method.

"But your parents were hippies back in the olden days,"

I said. "They must do something irregular. If they don't walk on their hands, do they ever levitate?"

"What?"

"Some of those hippies were interested in a swami that came from India and made millions of dollars teaching people to relax and stop caring about war and so on. If they got really good in his particular kind of meditation, they could start learning to levitate. As long as there weren't any newspaper reporters or photographers around."

"Levitate?"

"That means rise from the floor or the earth and hover in the air," said Professor Purzelbaum. "No one on earth has ever done it. Get it?"

"Ho ho."

"Haw haw."

"Hee hee."

"Five no trump," said Feet.

We sat in silence for a while. I can't say for sure what the others were thinking, but I was trying to think of something else Feet's parents might do that normal people don't do.

"Well," said Feet. "I thought of something, but it's probably way too far out to count."

We all leaned toward her. People at the next table leaned toward her. The waitress leaned toward her. I saw someone on the street out front peering in the window, his face against the glass and his hands around his forehead to see past the morning reflection. That was probably a coincidence. There was another guy right beside him, who looked just like him and was doing the same thing. That was no coincidence.

"Take a chance and tell us, Ms Feet."

Harry said that.

"My father can blow air out of his ear," said Feet.

"There you *go*," said the waitress, slapping the check down on the only bare part of the table top.

Feet's father was what people call an executive. If you work with your hands on stuff, you get called by a noun. So you're a tree faller or a baker or a goldsmith. If you talk on the telephone and wear a dark suit and understand what preferred shares and futures are, you get called by an adjective. By an abstract adjective. An executive.

He worked in a tall black glass building right in the middle of downtown. My father told me once that when he was young you could smell the ocean right downtown. Now with all those black glass buildings all you can smell is cars and buses.

Professor Purzelbaum parked the orange Gremlin next to a sign with a circled and crossed out capital P, and we all squeezed out.

"What floor?" I asked when we got into the huge lobby with the ceiling far far above our heads.

"Forty-one," said Feet, pushing the elevator button.

"I was afraid of that," I admitted.

I hate those elevators that zoom you up thirty floors before they stop. And I hate being thirty or forty floors up anyway. When I'm up there I can feel the building swaying. I want to grab a handrail or something, because I can feel my feet slipping sideways. I detest looking out a window and seeing clouds. Once when I flew with my parents to Toronto, and we were descending, the flight attendant referred to it as our final approach. I didn't like that. It was worse than when we were told just before the flight that we would be taking off momentarily. Why do they use such scary language when you are sitting there with white knuckles and toes digging holes in the soles of your shoes?

Anyway, on the descent, the pilot took a little circle tour so we could see what was happening just below us. There were two huge helicopters hovering, while idiotically brave workmen hammered in the long pointy top of the CN Tower. Here is what I said when I saw them doing that: "Boy, I'm glad I'm not up *there*!" Meanwhile I was sitting above them in a falling cylinder of aluminum.

But I could not remain behind while the rest of them went up to see Feet's father, and we could not very well ask an executive to come down to the ground floor. So up we went. I figured I would pick up my stomach on the way back down. Oh, I hated to think of how fast that little square room would go back down its shaft.

There was a somewhat wide but still really pretty woman sitting at a very high desk with two computers in front of her. First she tapped on one of the computers for long enough to type The quick brown fox jumps over the lazy dog. Then she asked us whether we had an appointment.

"I am Mr Corbishly's only daughter," said Feet, a phony dazzling smile on her face.

"A little more light on the teeth, please," I whispered close to Feet's ear as the woman tapped on her other computer.

"You can go in," she said. She sounded a little envious.

Mr Corbishly timed it so that just as we were entering his enormous office filled with vases loaded with flowers, he was getting to his feet and striding toward us, welcoming hand extended.

"Coriander!" he said, his face breaking into top and bottom. "How nice to see you down here in my playroom. And you brought your friends! Hello, Nevin!" He was looking at me when he said that, so I said hello.

Then he caught sight of Professor Purzelbaum. For a moment a look of nervousness washed over his face. But he was an executive, so he knew how to overcome such a problem, and he knew he was never supposed to look as if he weren't on top of the situation. He did up his suit jacket button.

We introduced my role model.

"Well, what brings you four—you five—to the pulse of the city?"

Executives like to talk their special kind of jive talk when they are talking to kids or professors. It seems to make it look as if they were being friendly on your level, but you were supposed to notice that they couldn't quite manage to get that far down.

Now I know why Feet had been sleeping on the floor at my place. I could not bring myself to imagine three or four of these Mr Corbishlys. I mean, he *is* my friend's father, but–

Of course, we were wondering whether he *was* the original Mr Corbishly.

"I don't know whether you will believe us," said Feet, "but we came down to hear you blow air out of your ear."

Mr Corbishly stared at her for a few seconds. Then he stared at the rest of us, about three seconds each.

"The last person I did that for disappeared, sort of," he said.

"What?"

"What?"

"Huh?"

"What?"

"Sort of?"

Mr Corbishly looked over both shoulders. Then he went to his desk and snapped a switch. Then he came back and gestured that we should come with him to the farthest corner of his office. I hated that part because the farthest corner of his office was where two windows came together at right angles, and through those windows I could see that we were far too high above the tiny cars in the narrow little streets below us.

I maneuvered so that I could keep as many of the other people as possible between me and the windows.

"You know those other, uh, grownups? Those us-people?" he said, looking over his shoulder. An eagle flew by and he jumped a little.

"Parents from space," chirped Viv.

"Shhhh!"

"What's the matter?" asked Harry. It was the first time he had spoken. I think he was in a kind of awe here in this fancy office forty-one floors above Oyster Street. He had his yellow rain hat in his hands.

"An executive vice-president cannot have creatures from outer space living at his house," said Mr Corbishly.

"That's understandable," said Professor Purzelbaum.

"So who disappeared when you did the ear trick, Pop?" asked Feet.

"Don't call me Pop," he said.

"Don't call me Coriander," she said.

"That's your name," he said.

"I know a kid named Krishna Sunflower Gottlieb," she said. "He goes by the name of Rudy. His parents used to put incense sticks in his lunch kit."

I didn't even know that was Rudy's real name. I'm glad my parents were never very serious citizens of the Age of Aquarius.

"So what happened?" persisted Feet.

Her father lowered his voice to an executive whisper.

"One of the other people who look like me found me in the garden cutting back the *ipomoea*."

"That's a morning glory," said the Professor.

"You might say," said the Executive. "Anyway, we

started talking, and I don't recall how the subject came up, but I told him about how I could blow air out my ear. He laughed. So I got him to lean in close and listen. He did, and I let a good loud stream of air out my ear."

"I think I know what happened then," said Professor Purzelbaum.

Feet's father looked at him with doubt.

"Air came out of *his* ear," said the Prof, "and everything else."

"Exactly! He just took off like a balloon with the string untied. Came down somewhere behind the *echinops*."

"Globe thistle," said our scientist.

"Right. I didn't stop to look for him, or it. I just hightailed it into the house and got my tennis racket and left for the Balsam Club."

There was a silence all at once in the room. We could hear a telephone ringing in the reception room.

"Mr Corbishly," said Professor Purzelbaum. "Would you mind showing us your ear trick?"

Mr Corbishly closed his mouth tight, closed his eyes, pinched his nose with his thumb and forefinger, and leaned his head down. We all leaned in, like a small football team in a huddle. Mr Corbishly blew air out of his ear.

"Phew!" said Professor Purzelbaum.

On the way down in the elevator I had my eyes closed, but I heard what Feet told Professor Purzelbaum.

"Oh I think I would have known if he wasn't my real father."

Here it was midnight again and here we were one more time at the Thunderdog Neighbourhood Pub parking lot. We were going to do more research. Professor Purzelbaum had gone inside to make sure that Mr Dropo was doing the favour they had agreed on the night before. Now he was coming out the door and down the steps. It was a good thing a neighbourhood policeman didn't come by. He might not have believed that this was the way Professor Purzelbaum always looked and that that was the way he always walked down a flight of stairs.

But there was nothing to worry about in that regard. Like I said, when people are coming out of a beer parlour and somehow getting into their cars, there is never a police person within a kilometer of the place. That works on the same principle as 41st Avenue. The speed limit on 41st Avenue is the same as the speed limit all over town, but more than half the drivers use it as a race track. You can drive up and down 41st Avenue all day and you will never see anyone getting a speeding ticket from a police person.

But I am wandering off the point. My mother and my Social Studies teacher Mr Dunham always tell me I am wandering off the point. Once I tried to defend myself by saying that I was just trying to live like the French movie I had seen, called *Moderato Cantabile*. But my mother just said she would Cantaloupe me, and Mr Dunham just said I was digressing because I didn't know the answer.

I went to that movie with Viv and Feet. Harry was up the street, watching *Destry Rides Again*. Viv didn't like the movie all that much.

"A woman takes a long long looonnnnnnngg walk and we watch her from a distance and there isn't even any music like there would be in an American movie to tell us what we are supposed to be feeling about all this."

"Yes," I said, "but–"

"A man and a woman in a cafe sit and talk for *hours* with faint droning voices, and all the while the camera closes in on a salt shaker," said Viv, throwing her arms above her head.

We were walking along Kaiser Street. As so often happened, people were ducking to get out of Viv's way. She is the most enthusiastic person I know. I hope she doesn't go into business, selling stuff and all.

I mean her movie reviews are either dynamite raves or devastating axe jobs. She never thinks anything is just okay. If she was a Social Studies teacher she would give you an A on your examinations, or an F. You would never get a C+ off of Viv.

C+ is what I get in most things. Even in band. You would think they would give me the benefit of the doubt because there is no such thing as a left-handed tuba, so I have to play it with my weak hand. No such luck. They said I could have gone into something where left-handedness didn't matter, like the bass drum or the triangle.

The triangle. I am a tuba player, the modest aristocrat of the marching band. But with a double B-flat tuba it isn't often that you are going to play *moderato cantabile*. *Moderato cantabile* means moderately fast with a flowing melodic feeling. Basically we tuba players go bum-BUM bum-BUM bum-BUM.

Feet was, as she often was, quiet and seemingly thoughtful. When Viv stopped for a breath, I asked Feet how she felt about *Moderato Cantabile*. She said she thought it was a pace-setting movie.

"What?" asked Viv, so loudly that heads turned a block in front of us. I steered us into Flics, and signalled to Guido that we would find our own table, near the back. There were about six people in the place, all of whom we had seen at the theatre.

"Pace-setting," repeated Feet.

"The only pace I saw was slow slow sloooooooowww," said Viv, gesturing and knocking a serviette-dispenser clattering across the floor.

"Ground-breaking," said Feet.

"Well," I said, "I sort of fall between your two positions. I would have to give it three and a half stars."

"Stars?" asked Feet, quietly, and turning to give me a glance mixed of surprise and low regard. "Since when do we start giving stars to movies? I thought we were film reviewers, not TV guide touts."

"What's a tout?" asked Guido, as he disbursed three cappuccinos with cinnamon on the fluffy stuff.

What's disbursed, you might ask.

Well, I look up a new word in the dictionary every day, and use it all day, and that way I memorize at least 365 new words a year. Today I learned feckless. A neat word. I plan to use it around Harry for the next few days.

Speaking of Harry, he came into Flics right about then, wearing a big cowboy hat as befits the movie he had just come from. He shouted out his order—a pumpkin and apricot soda—and sat down with us, sitting backward in his ice cream chair and tipping his hat back with his thumb. I knew we were going to be in for Destry all evening.

"How was your movie, Ma'am?" he asked Feet.

"Neville gave it stars," she said, in a monotone.

Come to think of it, I wonder why it's always stars. Why don't we rate things with moons, or triangles, or bulldozers?

"I'll have to give this novel three and a half bulldozers, Chuck. It's pretty strong on plot and setting, but it is certainly no pace-setting book."

"I'm afraid I have to disagree with you, Clarence. I'm going to give it one and a half tea pots. The characters were sketchy and the chapters were too long. I like to read one chapter while I'm having my toast and grapefruit in the morning, and I couldn't get through more than half a chapter on this book. One and a half tea pots."

I hope you understand that Chuck and Clarence are figments of my imagination. But then maybe I'm a figment of *your* imagination. Remember Harry's problem with whether we are all characters in a movie? The way I look at it, there really isn't any difference between Chuck and Clarence, say, and you and me.

Or let me put it this way: is there really such a thing as a digression, I mean wandering off the point? For some people, wandering off the point might be what other people would call getting closer to the point. You don't have to be from outer space to understand that.

Now, where was I? Oh yes, I was in Flics with my movie associates. Or was I in the parking lot of the Thunderdog Neighbourhood Pub with my planet-saving colleagues and the Professor of distant stellar facts? Or was I at home some time after this, writing words in a scribbler I was supposed to be using in Social Studies? What would Mr Dunham say if I handed in this for my assignment on foreign affairs?

You will see that when you start one of these things you can get awfully mixed up about time, not to mention space.

"Oh no," I said out loud.

"What?"

"Huh?"

"I beg your pardon."

"Oh no," I said. "What if these extra moms and dads are not only from outer space but also from the future?"

Feet gave me what they call a withering stare.

"What possible difference could that make?" she asked.

She had me there. At least I thought she had me there. It was at this point that Harry penetrated the conversation with some good sense. Every once in a while he will look up at you from one of his weird drinks and say something so smart you are glad he's your friend.

"It might not make much difference to us," Harry said. "But it could make all the difference in the world to them."

"Hmm," said Feet.

"All the difference in the world. Get it? Ah ha ha ha," said Harry.

I punched him on the shoulder. Viv kicked him in the shin. Feet gave him a withering stare.

"Explain, Mr Fieldstone," I said.

"Call me Destry."

"I'll Destry you," I threatened. Oh oh.

Harry leaned on the hood of a shiny silver Japanese sedan. He crossed his arms in front of him. He turned his air force wedge cap back to front. We leaned toward him.

"If they are from another galaxy in the present, they can presumably just go back where they came from. But if they are from the future there's no way they can go back as far as I can see," said Harry.

"Why not?" asked Viv. What's the difference between space and time?"

"A good question," said Harry.

We leaned further.

"How's about a good answer?" I requested.

"You're sure I'm not wandering off the point?"

Feet balled up a fist and held it quietly in front of Harry's face.

"Well," he said. "I think you can go back in time because all that stuff has happened, so you just go back the way you got here, kind of in the footprints you made getting to where you are now."

"A cute analogy, but probably full of holes," said Feet.

"Hmm. Well, I don't think you can go to the future, because it hasn't happened yet. There aren't any footprints."

"What about the footprints they made getting back here?" asked Viv.

"Well, sure," said Harry. "But now they are here in the present. The world they came from hasn't happened yet."

"Then how can they be here?" asked Viv. "I mean if they came from a place that hasn't happened, how can they have happened?"

"Maybe they haven't," said Harry.

"That's crazy," said Viv. "And I don't want to hear any more. It makes my head hurt, and it is impossible, anyway."

"Wait," I said. "I think Harry might be on to something."

"Oh sure," said Feet. "A left-handed tuba player gives his approval."

But Harry wasn't finished.

"Oh no, wait a minute. I just thought of something."

"Hooray!" whispered Feet.

"It has to do with what Viv asked. What's the difference between time and space? I mean space is what we can measure if we have time, and time is what it takes to measure space. They are just aspects of each other. That's what it says in the first chapter of our science text."

"Ugh!" whispered Viv.

"So," I said.

Harry put his wedge cap on frontward.

"Exactly," said Harry. "What it suggests to me is that either they can't get back to where they came from because it is not now there now—or they aren't here now any more than they would have been if they were from the future."

"Then what are we waiting in a dark parking lot for?" asked Viv.

"We're waiting for Professor Purzelbaum to see how many Mr Dropos there are in there," said Harry.

22.

"Here he comes now," said Harry.

Professor Purzelbaum stumbled a bit coming down the concrete steps from the door of the Thunderdog, and he knocked his feet together once while crossing the parking lot to where we were, leaning against the orange Gremlin.

"How many?" asked Viv.

"Three!" he announced.

We had all thought there would be just two Mr Dropos, the original and one space clone. But apparently the remaining aliens had both taken to Mr Dropo's hobby, the emptying of beer glasses.

"Will that affect our plans?" I asked.

I was not really too clear on what our plans were. I think we were supposed to be finding out something scientific and something military. Well, military isn't the right word, but something useful in the possible war of the worlds. Well, war of the worlds isn't quite the right phrase, but it is a neat title.

The scientific question was about motivation. Why were the visitors here? Where did they come from, and why did they leave home, and how come they came here, of all places in the universe? Professor Purzelbaum had brought a little portable tape recorder, and Harry was ready to grab it and turn it on if Professor Purzelbaum had trouble operating it.

The military question was about deflation. Why did parents from space once in a while fly through the air and come down empty like a limp balloon? We had found out that the "remains" disappeared after a few hours, except for the clothes they had been wearing. The police didn't want to tell us that, but Professor Purzelbaum got on the telephone and pretty soon there was a man in uniform whispering in his ear. My role model was looking better all the time, despite the hair and ears and glasses.

The second half of the military question was about

procedure. If we found out what made an alien deflate, what were we going to do? Would we deflate them all? Or would we threaten to deflate them all unless they went back home or took off to find another planet with kids on it?

I figured they should be looking for a planet of orphans.

Here was the main moral question: is it all right to deflate an artificial parent even if that artificial parent has not done anything that will threaten life and limb? Here is the other half of the main moral question: is there anything wrong with deflating an idea? Here is the second half of that second half: are they just ideas that someone somewhere else has, and therefore no great loss if they have other ideas? Or are the ideas the main life force? I mean are the ideas all the creatures are? If we knock off an idea are we committing homicide as well as ideocide?

And here I was, just a kid. I shouldn't have to handle these heavy problems. That's what school counsellors and social workers on radio phone-in programs are for.

"Here we go," said Viv.

The doors were opening, and clumsy people were coming out. Some were singing. Some had their arms around the shoulders of their lifelong friends. Some were trying hard to do up their jacket buttons or zippers. Some were shouting that they remembered where they had left their cars. The nearest traffic cop was on another continent.

And finally, there was Mr Dropo, followed by Mr Dropo, and there a few people behind them was Mr Dropo. We all walked forward to meet them.

"Hello, Mr Dropo. Remember us? The Mayflies?"

"It does?" asked the nearest Mr Dropo.

"No, no," said Harry. "We are a kind of ephemeral insect called a Mayfly. I mean in terms of your years. I mean the long time you—"

"Dough know what you're talking about," said the nearest Mr Dropo. Then he hiccuped, and we stepped back a bit, just in case.

So I figured that he had to be the real Mr Dropo, if I can still use that term. I turned to one of the others. He was standing with his arms hanging straight down, his shirt out on one side, and a big smile on his face.

"We have come to take you all for coffee and dough-nuts," I said.

"Beer!" said the third Mr Dropo.

"Coffee and doughnuts," said Viv with a smile in her voice.

"And carrot cake," said Harry "Or raisin pie. Blueberry muffins, maybe. Butterhorns, prune Danish—"

"Pipe down, Harry," said Feet.

"Beer!" said the Mr Dropo with his shirt half out.

Professor Purzelbaum leaned over and spoke in what appeared to be the original Mr Dropo's ear. Professor Purzelbaum thought he was whispering, but he appeared unable to. I heard his half-shout.

"Remember our deal?" he half-shouted. "Let's get them over to Kliks."

"Flics," I said.

"Follow me," said Mr Dropo.

There were only two customers in Flics when we arrived, probably the last couple dawdling behind the after-movie crowd. He was wearing an earring shaped like a parrot, and a head scarf covered with pictures of Mickey Mouse. She was wearing a short leather skirt and black stockings with holes in them. Her face was dead white and her lipstick was purple.

When they saw four kids, a man in a lab coat with a haystack on his head, and three big beer guys that looked like each other, they got up and left without finishing their cappuccinos. Harry looked at the cappuccinos and thought it over for a second, then decided not to finish them.

Guido was not ecstatic to see such a crowd, but we were eight potential customers, so he chattered his welcomes as he pushed two tables together, and we all managed to sit in separate chairs. Guido stood near the table, his order pad in one hand and his pen in the other.

"Eight coffees and sixteen doughnuts," said Professor Purzelbaum.

"Make that seven coffees and one rosehip tea," said Harry.

"Seven coffees and one rosehip tea and sixteen doughnuts," said Guido happily.

"Fourteen doughnuts and two apple fritters," said Harry.

146

"Harry?" asked Feet.

"Yes, my dove?"

"Pipe down, Harry. Pipe. Down."

"Don't be feckless, Harry," I added.

When the coffee had arrived and the doughnuts were piled on two large plates, one on each table, Professor Purzelbaum put his little tape recorder on the table top and poked at it with his long bony finger.

"Now, I understand that two of you fellows are from another orb," he said, poking away.

Harry reached over and pushed the record and play buttons, and the little tape started turning.

"Orb?" asked the real Mr Dropo, I think.

"He isn't really addressing you," said Feet. "I think."

"Orb?" asked another Mr Dropo.

"Planet," said Professor Purzelbaum.

The three Mr Dropos filled their mouths with doughnut and poured coffee in after it. A lot of people eat doughnuts that way. If people from another orb do it, too, maybe that is the natural, universal, interstellar way to consume coffee and doughnuts. I know just what my grandmother would say to such a proposition. I know what my mother would say, too.

"I am from the planet Earth, and my name is Bladdermear Dropo," said one of the aliens, I think.

The other alien leaned over and whispered something in his ear, but there was not a sound. The leaning was probably for show. I think he just sent a thought to the other alien. A light bulb.

"Vladimir Dropo, I mean," said the latter.

"That's me," said Mr Dropo.

Guido came over and filled the coffee cups. That was something he never did in ordinary circumstances. He did not go far from our table either, certainly not out of earshot, as they say. Being Ukrainian, he was probably interested to hear the name Vladimir. Or maybe this was the first time he had ever seen triplets.

On the wall the giant poster face of Marlon Brando looked a little amazed himself.

"Excuse me," Feet interjected. "But we were talking with one of you in the park a couple nights ago, and whichever one it was admitted to us that he was from another world deep in space."

"Oh, that was 285ZOF.7," said one of the visitors.

"No no," said the other one. "That was Vladimir."

"Aha!" said Professor Purzelbaum, and pointed his long bony finger at the tape recorder. "We've got that on tape right here."

His finger hit the off button. Harry turned it back on.

"Aha!" said Guido, waving the coffee pot around. But the cups were all full already.

"You aren't really part of this investigation, Guido," I said.

"I'll throw in two free chocolate doughnuts each if they confess," said Guido.

"We two are from another planet," said one of the visitors. "So was 285ZOF.7, but he deflated."

"What?" asked Harry.

"Deflated."

There was a silence. I think we movie reviewers were all wondering whether we were supposed to mourn the passing of the artificial Mr Dropo we had spoken with in the park. I remembered how he had disappeared as if he was just a dream, or an idea. So why weren't these two disappearing?

"When we were speaking with him the other night he just disappeared all of a sudden," I said.

"We can all do that," said the visitor with his shirt out.

"So why don't you?" asked Viv.

"We're getting free doughnuts," he said. "And we like the company. Mr Dropo, for instance, bought every round at the Thunderdog Neighbourhood Pub."

Professor Purzelbaum was supposed to be leading this research, but he was too patient for me. His method seemed to be to sit back and listen to whatever anyone said. I mean they might have started discussing the weather or the latest baseball scores. I wanted to get to things that mattered.

"Where are you from?" I asked.

"You aren't going to believe this, but we come from a planet we call Earth."

"Wait a minute," said Viv very loudly. "Are you translating now? Do you say the sound of 'Earth' when you say it to each other, or do you say something that translates to 'Earth' when you're speaking English?"

One of the visitors screwed up his Mr Dropo face and thought for a second or two. Then he tried an answer.

"Well, that's hard to say, really. You see, the language we speak to each other we call English."

"Great. Just great," said Feet.

"Doughnuts!" said the real Mr Dropo.

"But are you just translating that as 'English'?" asked Viv.

"I suppose you could say that," replied the visitor. "But if we translated your language into what we speak, we would call it 'English'."

"But you are translating that right now, aren't you?" asked Viv.

"Either that or the other way around," admitted the visitor.

"Wait, wait! I can't follow this," said Guido, a pot of coffee in his hand.

"You aren't in this research, Guido," Feet reminded him.

I pointed at the tape recorder and pointed at the visiting Mr Dropos and wiggled my eyebrows up and down at Professor Purzelbaum.

"Oh yeah," he said. He pushed the little tape recorder closer to one of the visitors. "One thing we would like to know," he said, sounding like a bad imitation of a CBC interviewer, "is why you decided to come here."

The visiting Mr Dropo put on a special tone, sounding like a bad imitation of someone being interviewed on the CBC.

"Well, you see, it looked like a pretty nice town. Lots of trees. An ocean nearby. Good schools, and lots of parks. A low crime rate, we heard."

"No no. Back up," said Professor Purzelbaum. "Let's talk in broader terms. How come you decided to come to the planet Earth?"

"We started from the planet Earth."

Feet sighed loudly.

"Oh yes," said Professor Purzelbaum. He leaned toward the tape recorder. "Okay, let's try to establish the reasons why you came to this particular planet Earth."

"Well, wouldn't you?" asked the second visiting Mr Dropo.

"I certainly would," said Harry. "Where else could you get a sour cherry cola with your tuna melt?"

Viv showed him her first and second fingers and indicated his eyeballs. He returned to his doughnut. He had an annoying way of picking little pinches off his doughnut and eating a pinch at a time.

"All right," said Professor Purzelbaum. "Perhaps we should come at this question from the other end. Tell us why you left your home planet in the first place."

"Earth."

"Yes, why did you leave your original planet Earth?"

The two imitation Mr Dropos glanced at each other. They were quiet for a while. So were we all, even Harry. Even Guido, who was pretending to wipe the surface of a nearby table. Then the two imitation Mr Dropos began to speak at once. Then they both stopped. Then the real Mr Dropo opened his mouth to say something. Then he looked at the glaring eyes of Feet and Viv, and returned to his coffee.

Professor Purzelbaum put his long bony fingers on the arm of the tweed jacket worn by the nearer alien.

"Tell us," he said, "in your own words."

Viv squeezed her eyes tight at that expression.

Guido filled the coffee cups.

"Well," said the Mr Dropo, "It started with overpopulation."

"Yep, overpopulation," said the other one.

"We've got that in places," said Harry.

"Too many people," said the first Mr Dropo.

"Way too many, it turned out," said the second Mr Dropo.

"So we passed a law saying no more children."

"Sounds like a great law," said Guido.

"Ahem!" shouted Viv.

"Wait, wait, wait!" pleaded Harry. "If you are just ideas–"

"*Just* ideas?"

"Okay, if you are ideas–"

"That's your term, of course,"

"If you are something like what we call ideas," said Harry, with mock patience, "how can you have an overpopulated planet. How could you use up all the available room?"

"Subtract a 117 from 44," said one Mr Dropo.

"Name twenty stars in this galaxy," said the other Mr Dropo.

"What is the difference between a restrictive clause and a non-restrictive clause?"

"What are the inert gases and what are their atomic numbers?"

"Wait wait, one thing at a time," pleaded Harry.

"We rest our case," said one of the Mr Dropos.

"Well, you passed a law against the population explosion. So how did you expect to keep the race alive?" I asked.

The two foreign Mr Dropos looked at one another for a moment, as if debating telepathically whether to explain it to me. Then they both started at once. Then the second Mr Dropo deferred to the third Mr Dropo.

"We didn't have to worry about that," said the latter. "Ideas never really die, and we are mainly ideas. At least that is the only way I can explain it to you. So we didn't have children because we needed them to keep the race, as you put it, alive. We would just have children because we like them so much."

"I thought so," said Professor Purzelbaum, making sure that his words would be picked up by the tape recorder.

What a neat role model.

"Yes, but then the planet got full, and we passed a law saying no more children."

"You can imagine how some people felt when their kids had all grown up," said the other foreign Mr Dropo. "Young ideas, so to speak, are so nice to have around. That's when people started listening to 933TTY.4."

"What?"

"What?"

"Who?"

"Huh?"

"933TTY.4. She said she had a plan to rove the universe and find a planet full of children. I mean for people who just couldn't live without them. It was a terrifically popular idea, or rather she was."

"Oh dear," said Harry.

"Most of the folks on the planet wanted to go on the expedition. But so far there is just the one vessel, an experiment, really. We are among the lucky folks who got to go on the search."

"So at last you found Earth, or at least our version of Earth," said Viv, illumination all over her face and eyes. What a glow, a flash. I took off my glasses and wiped them where I had touched them with my doughnut fingers.

"Oh we found several planets with children on them. Yours was the first one with such a nice city beside the ocean where you didn't have to worry about sunburn all that much."

"So you studied us," said Professor Purzelbaum. He sounded like the detective who is just about to reveal the identity of the murderer.

"Correct," said the first foreign Mr Dropo. "We studied you and formed these shapes to walk around in. Our main method is, of course, visual observation."

"But once in a while—"

"Well, as you have seen, once in a while there is something that someone did not observe, and the idea can't hold on to the person."

"We have the opposite problem," I said.

"Ahem!" Viv reminded me.

"So your friend 28-something isn't dead?" said Feet.

"285ZOF.7. Oh, heavens, no. He's back up in the vessel, thinking about it."

"Do I detect a rule here?" asked Professor Purzelbaum.

"Exactly. Anyone who deflates here doesn't get a second chance unless we go to another planet."

"How cruel!" said Viv.

"Not at all. He's still alive. He just doesn't get to be a father any more. He isn't in any worse shape than the people back on Earth."

"Your Earth, you mean?" said Harry.

"Exactly. Home. Ah."

Professor Purzelbaum turned his head quickly toward the second foreign Mr Dropo, who had just said those words. Then he used one long bony finger to push his glasses back up his nose. They descended right away.

24.

After the real Mr Dropo fell asleep with his head tilted back and his mouth wide open, we realized that it was time to get him home to bed. He had to go to work in the morning at the offices of McCray, McCray, Tollinson and

Farquahar, Barristers and Solicitors. At least that's what he said before he nodded off. I always thought he was a butcher.

Guido was in no hurry to close. Usually when we sit there past eleven fifty-five at night, he will be cleaning tables and sweeping the floor in a way that we cannot mistake. Tonight he was all ears and free coffee. But we had to get Mr Dropo home. I wasn't even starting to think about how I was going to get us four adventurers into my house without bringing down the wrath of the warlords. I would just hope that my father was sitting up alone, watching the late movie or reading a locomotive magazine.

So there the eight of us were, standing on the sidewalk in front of Flics, the way people do. Viv was trying to brush doughnut crumbs off Harry's jacket. The grownups were saying good night to each other. I took the tape recorder from Professor Purzelbaum's hand and turned it off for him and shoved it into the pocket of his lab coat while he talked with the triplets. I think he was trying to set up another meeting for further research.

I remembered the look that crossed his face when he heard the space visitor sighing about home.

I caught sight of my head in the window of the women's skimpy underwear store next to Flics. My hair was sticking out straight to one side. I hate it when my hair sticks out to the side or straight up. It's not as if I spend twenty minutes in the school washroom trying to make every hair contribute to a ravishing male beauty, the way some guys do. But I don't want to look like a goof either. At least as far as my hair is concerned. It's bad enough that my ears stick straight out. I don't want my hair to join them.

I took off my glasses and held them by the end of one of the ear things between my teeth. Then I took out my comb, and using the window of the underwear store for a mirror, started combing my hair.

One of the Mr Dropos deflated.

There was a definite whoosh of air, and the envelope of human clothes went in loops and dives and soaring climbs out over the middle of the street. At least I think that's what happened. By the time I got my glasses on the clothes were lying human-shaped on the pavement. Luckily there wasn't a lot of traffic, but one huge dark American car screeched and fishtailed and came to rest at an angle to the sidewalk.

A drunk man about twenty-two years old clambered out.

"Did I hit him?" he asked, his eyes wild.

"It's just a bunch of clothes," said Viv.

"Stupid place for a bunch of clothes," said the drunk guy, and started getting back into his big car.

"You shouldn't be driving," said Viv.

"Aw, I can drive when I can't walk," he said.

His car banged into a parked car and a newspaper box while he was straightening it out. I was hoping a police car would drive by, but no such luck.

We all gathered around the flat rind of the gone Mr

Dropo and kind of shoved it with our feet. No one wanted to pick it up so we shoved it with our feet to the curb.

Later in the middle of the night some guy would come along and see those free clothes there. If he got there late enough it would just be clothes. If he got there too early he would get a surprise when he saw the flat skin of a Mr Dropo fading away.

"Now why do you suppose that happened?" murmured Professor Purzelbaum.

"Beats me," said the real Mr Dropo. "I am not sure I even know exactly what happened."

"You kids, was any of you doing anything unusual?" asked the Prof.

"I was just brushing leftover food off Harry. That's pretty usual," said Viv.

"I was just standing there looking at Neville," said Feet. "He was staring his eyeballs out at the lacy-bow underwear in the window of Monsieur Jack's."

"I was not especially looking at underwear," I objected. "I was just using any window that happened to be there."

"What for?" asked Professor Purzelbaum.

"I was combing my hair," I said.

"Nothing unusual about that," said Harry. "Either you are combing your hair or it is sticking out to the side. You should get a hat."

The two Mr Dropos had their arms around each other's shoulders. It was a good thing they had some coffee and doughnuts in their stomachs. It looked as if they were consoling each other.

"Poor 901YUL.0," said one of them. "He's going to wake up with a hangover in the vessel."

"Can an idea have a hangover?" asked Professor Purzelbaum.

"I don't know," said the apparently artificial Mr Dropo. "We never had a hangover before we came to this lovely planet."

"I've never had a hangover, and I've lived here all my life," said Harry.

The face of the empty Mr Dropo was looking at me. I went around behind Professor Purzelbaum so I wouldn't have to look back. I had to remind myself that what's-his-number was asleep up in the interstellar vessel, if you can say that ideas can sleep. Ideo-persons, let's say. I looked the other way. There was Guido's face staring from the darkened window of his cafe.

"I wonder what he saw that took the wind out of him," said my role model.

"Aha!"

That was Feet. She was usually not as loud as, say, Viv. I had never heard her say anything as loud as this. Maybe she was upset to see someone deflate, especially in the street.

"What is it, Toe?" asked Professor Purz.

"Neville was combing his stupid hair."

"At least I'm not wearing sandals," I said. I was sensitive about my hair, as you know.

"Left-handed," said Feet.

"Big deal," I said. "I have been combing my hair left-handed for years and years. There's nothing unusual about that."

Professor Purzelbaum parted his cascade of straw-hair and pushed his glasses up his nose and leaned down and peered at me, as if he were trying to see something peculiar in my construction.

"Maybe combing your hair left-handed is usual for you," he whispered loudly. "But maybe they never thought of that."

He dipped his head toward the remaining space Dropo.

We all started walking along Kaiser Street, more or less in the direction of the orange Gremlin. The Mr Dropos still had their arms around each other's shoulders, and sometimes they stepped on each other's shoes. We passed the Smedley Theatre where *Teenage Microwave Murders III* was announced as the coming attraction.

"Aha!"

Except for the Mr Dropos and Viv, we all jumped. Viv was the one who had shouted Aha.

"Everyone in Neville's family is left-handed," she shouted.

"Even the canary," said Feet, sarcastically.

"He's a budgie," I said.

We stopped walking and formed a clump of people in front of a store with nothing inside. There were a thousand advertisements for musical events and miracle diets pasted onto the windows. There was one hightop basketball shoe lying in the doorway.

"A family of left-handed people," murmured the astronomer.

"The only kid in our group that didn't get extra parents," said Harry, turning his wedge cap around sideways.

"Mr Dropo, we'd like to talk with you some more," said Professor Purzelbaum.

He tugged and tugged at his pocket, until he finally got the little tape recorder out. Then he pushed all the buttons, including rewind, so I took it and fast-forwarded, and listened, and got the tape to the place at which we had left off. What a bother.

The real Mr Dropo and the imitation Mr Dropo sat down together on a bench at a bus stop.

"Shoot," said the real one.

"Commence firing," said the artificial one.

I looked hard at his skin. I could not tell, at least in the street lamp light, any difference between it and the skin on Mr Dropo. There were no seams. But I knew that the features and colors would just fade away in a few hours if he deflated.

We gathered in a semi-circle in front of the bench, like a football huddle. Some of us were standing in the gutter.

"Do you know why your friend deflated?" asked Professor Purzelbaum. He was holding the tape recorder in front of the two men, though he was holding the microphone toward himself.

"Not a clue," said one of them.

"You mean 901YUL.0?" asked the other.

"Yes, good old 901," I said.

"We never call our friends by nicknames," said the alien Mr Dropo.

"Well, do you know what he saw that made him give up the ghost?" asked our Prof.

"I don't have a clue. It happens when we see human beings do something we didn't think they did, something we weren't programmed to imitate. If we want to make the idea flesh, so to speak, we have to get the flesh exactly right. At least that's the idea."

"We figured that," said Professor Purzelbaum.

"We did?" added Harry.

A police car drove by us very slowly. In fact it nearly came to a stop. There was a policewoman on our side of the blue car with the white stripe. She looked too small to be a police person. She stared at us hard, and the policeman to her left, a guy with a neck as wide as his head and a short black mustache, stared at us hard too. A car went by the other way about twenty kilometers an hour over the speed limit, probably driven by a guy who had just finished six hours at a bar. The two police persons looked hard at us, and then drove away, very slowly. I guess they were the bus stop patrol.

I like police people pretty well. I like them a lot better than criminal people. I just wish they would smile sometimes, the way they do in their advertising at school.

"Look," said Professor Purzelbaum to the friendly visitor. "If I can talk CJNK into it, will you appear on television with a couple of your fellow planet people?"

"Will we get paid?" asked the genial visiting Mr Dropo.

162

25.

I don't know whether you have ever seen a television show called "Mac," but I can tell you it is a kind of local version of those shows in which a loud-mouthed man or woman walks around the audience with a microphone and asks people embarrassing questions. I guess you've noticed that the people in the audience are always glad to answer the embarrassing questions. I think they are people who watch television all the time, and figure that at last they have been allowed across the threshold into a more important world. They are on television. They know just how to handle themselves because they have watched people just like them over and over again, talking about embarrassing things.

If they can't get on a game show, where they call everybody by their first name and clap their hands for everything including the commercials, they will settle for one of these shows about embarrassing things.

Well, the local one on CJNK had trouble finding embarrassing things all the time, because it was just local. So sometimes they would have a program about the school board or what people were hoping to get for Christmas.

Really gripping television. My mother usually managed to watch "Mac." It comes on at one or two in the afternoon.

It's called "Mac" because the guy with the microphone who jumps around in the audience is Mackenzie MacDonald, who is also the anchorman on the late news. When he is the anchorman on the late news he wears a suit and tie, or at least the top half of a suit and a tie. But on "Mac" he wears outfits that he thinks will make him seem up to date to the people he has on the show. If he has some loud teenage guitar players he wears blue jeans, but of course they have a crease in them. If he's talking with athletes who got caught using drugs he wears sweat pants and running shoes.

Now here he was hosting a program about parents from space. He was wearing corduroy pants, loafers with no socks, and a sweater made of about ten colours.

It would be better if they didn't call guests by their first names on this show, I was thinking. How will they manage with a guy named, say, 992HDL.4?

There was a panel of guests sitting in a row of chairs facing the audience. These were Mr Boudreau, the editor of the *Moon*, Professor Purzelbaum, the remaining extra Mr Dropo, one of the artificial Mr Corbishlys, and an extra mother from Harry Fieldstone's house. We four simple film critics were sitting in the front row of the audience. The audience was made up of what Mackenzie MacDonald called "A cross-section of the population." We were the only kids, though.

I noticed that Mackenzie MacDonald was wearing

makeup, some kind of stuff that made his skin light brown. No one else was wearing makeup, except for the extra Mrs Fieldstone. Maybe all the space visitors had to use makeup on their human skins.

I don't know why, but at first I had a hard time paying attention to what people were saying, and what was going on in general. I would kind of wake up when everything stopped while they ran a commercial. I guess I was imagining myself watching this on the set at home. I can't even look at an unplugged television set without having my mind wander.

Once in a while Viv would hit me in her excitement, and I would come to and hear the second half of a sentence. Viv is the kind of girl who jumps up and down while we are doing an experiment with beans and blotters in a science class.

"I am still not entirely convinced that this whole thing isn't a hoax being perpetrated by those four children who don't seem to have summer jobs. When I was their age a child was expected to get a summer job. Parents from right here on Earth were pretty important, and they could use a little help in keeping the household going...."

That was Mr Booboo from the *Moon*. I tuned out. When Viv hit me the next time, Professor Purzelbaum was answering a question.

"...so it appears that they deflate and fly off like an untied balloon when they see human beings doing something they did not think human beings did."

Professor Purzelbaum had seven pens clipped into the

breast pocket of his lab coat. A woman in the waiting room next to the television studio had come in and brushed his hair away from his face, but now it was falling in its usual way. I was glad.

"Like the soul departing the earthly body and ascending to heaven," suggested Mackenzie MacDonald. Then he stood up straight and looked around him, for the audience's approval of his perception and his sweater.

"Actually," said the visiting Mr Corbishly, "they just go back to the vessel."

"As ideas?"

"Well, that's *your* word."

"Then why," asked Mackenzie MacDonald, and he paused and smiled at his audience before he continued, "does an expedition of ideas require a space ship? Surely ideas can range freely across the universe?"

"They cannot take supplies," said the visiting Mr Corbishly. "Do you think we just dream up these human skins and suits of clothing?"

There was a murmur in the audience, which turned into a little ripple of laughter at the end. Mackenzie MacDonald grinned, hoping to make the audience his with its amusement.

He leaped past us and up the aisle a few rows. Then he stopped and looked dramatic for the camera.

"I understand that when you see a left-handed person you go phhhht!" he said, grinning more than I thought a person should.

The imitation Mr Dropo gestured toward me.

"I am looking at a left-handed person right now and here I remain, a complete tourist," he said.

"You are Mr Dropo?" asked Mackenzie MacDonald, rhetorically.

"Actually I am 771DMK.8," was the reply.

"All right, 771," said Mackenzie MacDonald, with a little smirk for his audience. "How come you aren't flying around like a dying balloon over our heads?"

He got a nice satisfying nervous laugh from his audience.

"I know about left-handed people now," said our Mr Dropo-like space person. "Though I must say that seemed the most difficult aberration to believe."

"Aberration, 771?"

"It was not too hard to accept blowing air from your ears, or walking on your hands or having ink-pictures on your arms. But left-handedness seems to run counter to the basic laws of nature."

Mackenzie MacDonald climbed higher in the audience.

"How many left-handers do we have here?"

Five people stuck up their left arms. I didn't bother, because I thought I had already been sufficiently identified.

Mackenzie MacDonald stuck his microphone in front of a left-handed woman's face.

"Do you think you're against the rules of nature?" he shouted.

The woman was about thirty years old. She wore

light-brown-rimmed glasses and had her light brown hair tied up in a bunch. She had hardly any makeup on. Her earth-colours sweater made her really attractive. She looked serious and gentle and seemed so sensible.

"Ask the people who make scissors," she said.

"Right on!" said another voice.

"Left on!" said a third.

"Excuse me," said Professor Purzelbaum, quite loudly.

I saw three cameras turn and aim at him. I saw Mackenzie MacDonald look annoyed for a second. Then I saw him skip down the stairs.

"Yes, Doctor Purzelbaum?" he said, his eyebrows lifted high.

Professor Purzelbaum's body leaned at a forty-five degree angle out of his chair and toward the audience.

"I am inclined to think we are getting off the topic," he said.

"The topic is outer space and left-handedness, as I see it," said the host of "Mac." He turned to the three aliens.

"I don't see how you can be left-handed," said the one who looked like Harry's mother.

"Why not?"

"Well, the universe doesn't work that way," she said.

Mackenzie MacDonald spun around once. Luckily he was carrying a cordless microphone.

"What do you mean, the universe?" His voice was half-way between a sneer and the false enthusiasm some grownups use when they are talking to little kids.

"Well, it goes counter-clockwise. Everyone knows

that," she said, and leaned back in her chair with her arms folded across her chest.

Mackenzie MacDonald was under the impression that he was winning now. He moved from the visiting Mrs Fieldstone to the visiting Mr Corbishly. I noticed Feet squirming beside me.

"What do clocks have to do with idea-people from across the galaxy?" our host, as he liked to be called, asked, as if he had caught the defense's star witness in a contradiction. "Surely you don't use the simple devices of measurement that are good enough for us mere Earthlings?"

"We use clocks."

"Whatever for?"

"Are you kidding? How else would we know when to get up and go to work?"

This is the point at which we four kids laughed out loud. We were the only ones laughing at first. Then row by row, the whole audience began a wave of laughter. This did not please Mackenzie MacDonald at all.

"You know, I think she's right," said Professor Purzelbaum. He seemed pretty excited. "That would fit everything we know so far, and it would explain some of the mysteries that have been dogging space physics for a decade!"

I looked at Mackenzie MacDonald. He looked bored. I looked at Mr Boudreau, the editor. He looked as if he wanted to be somewhere else.

"The discovery of the double helix was mind-boggling," said the excited Professor Purzelbaum. His glasses fell right off his nose and he caught them in one hand before they could reach the floor. I'm sure he didn't even notice. "But this is everything-boggling. This is double helix-boggling!"

We four kids clapped our hands loudly, and Harry whistled through his teeth. No one else applauded.

"Yes, well, I am certain that that is very interesting to your little group of specialists," said Mackenzie MacDonald with a fake chuckle. "But I think people watching at home are going to want to know more down to earth things, if you know what I mean. And we'll find them out after these important messages."

The cameramen stepped back and relaxed. A woman came dashing out of the darkness with a make-up brush and tissues and went to work on Mackenzie MacDonald's face. People in the audience talked with each other. I looked at Feet. She had a little shirt-pocket notebook open, and was trying to write in it left-handed.

"Aha," I whispered.

"I wonder if you can make your real parents deflate," she said. And then she looked up and flashed me a huge toothy smile.

"Ten seconds!" someone shouted.

I watched a woman with a clipboard hugged against her chest. She was holding up fingers and folding them down, from five to none.

"Hi! We're back," said Mackenzie MacDonald. "What is life like in a big space ship that has to spend years getting from solar system to solar system? We're going to find out on this segment of Mac."

He lunged up to the creature who looked like Harry's mother. If Harry weren't my friend, I would have to say that this extra parent of his was a pretty good-looking woman. Of course what we were looking at was a construct, a kind of duplication of Mrs Fieldstone. So as far as looks were concerned, we were looking at Mrs Fieldstone. Anyway, I guess I shouldn't say so, but she was pretty good-looking. She still is, if we're talking about the real Mrs Fieldstone. You know what I mean. I'm not sure I do, though.

Mackenzie MacDonald stood right in front of her and leaned over. He shot a look at the audience, flashed a television smile, and turned to his so-called guest.

"What about those long long nights on the space journey between your planet—what is it called?"

"We call it Earth," she said.

Some people in the audience snickered. Some gasped a little.

"Well, ha ha ha, I guess there's no patent on names for a planet," said Mackenzie MacDonald. "Now, getting to the nitty gritty—what did you do to wile away those long nights in outer space?"

There was a sweet motherly smile on her face.

"There is no such thing as night in outer space. No night, no day. Or if we put it another way—there is nothing but night, or nothing but day. You can't have night unless what we call the sun sets. And in outer space there isn't any sun. Well, there are lots of suns, but they are a long way away, and they don't look any bigger than your eye."

She sat back with her hands on her knees and smiled, just the way I have seen Harry's mother do dozens of times. I looked at Harry. He had his Culpepper Golf Club cap pulled down over his eyes, and he was slumped down in his seat.

I looked at Professor Purzelbaum. His hair was hanging over his eyes, and he was carrying his glasses in his hand. But his body looked alert. I didn't know whether he was paying sharp attention to the conversation or thinking about the counter-clockwise universe.

"Well," said Mackenzie MacDonald, moving on to the guest who looked like Mr Corbishly. "What I mean is— what is a space traveller's, uh, intimate life like?"

"Do you mean love?" asked the visitor.

"Well, I suppose you might put it that way," said the man in the makeup.

"Of course there is love. But we are in the normal course of things what we call ideomorphs. I believe you say idea-people. So our love is what you call Platonic."

"I am not sure that our viewers know what you mean," said Mackenzie MacDonald, still trying, against all the evidence, to sound superior.

"Oh, I keep forgetting; we are talking in front of television-watchers. Platonic love means a love like close soul-sharing friendship. That is the main form of love on Earth. I mean *our* planet Earth."

Mackenzie MacDonald stood on his tiptoes and then

came down and flexed his knees, and then stood straight with one leg in front of the other. He twirled his microphone for a bit, and then asked his question.

"Then how did you get into that trouble at home? I mean your group left to find space so you could have children. If Platonic love, as you call it, is the kind of love you get on your planet–let's call it Planet X–then, how did you get yourselves overpopulated?"

He thought he had him there.

"It started when everyone went crazy for Caesar salad."

"What?"

"What?"

"Huh?"

"Say again?"

Some of this dialogue was coming from the front row of the audience.

"Well, in order to make Caesar salad," continued the individual who resembled Mr Corbishly, "you have to have romaine lettuce. So when Caesar salad became the most fashionable diet item, everyone started growing romaine lettuce like mad. Well, as you know, the romaine lettuce patch is where children come from. You go out and lift a romaine lettuce leaf and there's another kid."

"Fantastic!" said Mackenzie MacDonald.

"Down here on Earth our parents always told us children came from the cabbage patch," said Mr Boudreau.

"Ho ho, that's a good one," said the creature that resembled Mrs Fieldstone.

"I get it," said Professor Purzelbaum. "With a counter-clockwise universe you get black holes and white dwarfs. With a clockwise universe we would have had white holes and black dwarfs."

"So by the time the Earth people decided to give up Caesar salad it was too late. There were kids all over the place. People had more kids than kids have parents in this town."

"But wait, wait," requested Mackenzie MacDonald. "Did you have Caesar? I mean to name the Caesar salad after?" His makeup was getting a little caked on his forehead.

"*Naturellement*. He was a famed polyp-ball player named 623HHU.0. In English you would say 'Caesar'. On Earth we call it 623HHU.0 salad."

"Or maybe white blacks and dwarf holes," said Professor Purzelbaum.

"I could go for a beer," said 771DMK.8.

"We'll be back right after this," said Mackenzie Mac-Donald.

The cameramen stepped back. The woman with the brush came out of the shadows. Feet got back up on her seat.

This time it was an old man counting down the seconds. He lifted one hand and started counting. He started with six.

The guest who looked like Mr Corbishly deflated above the heads of the audience.

Harry and Viv and Feet were afraid to go home now. I asked them whether they were aware of anything really bad done to any kids by any of the visiting parents. I told them that their own parents were probably getting a little browned off by now, and maybe *they* would be a little dangerous. I told them that I didn't know how long I was going to be able to escape the wrath of my own parents, not to mention my own extras, meaning my grandmother and my, ugh, sister.

All this explaining was to no avail. All three of them had this feeling that there was some big change coming up. I figured that maybe right-handed people had extra powers of perception, or maybe it was just that when you have lived in a house with four mothers and four fathers you know that something has to give.

So I had to switch my explaining to the members of my own family. For some reason, probably just chance encounter, I had to start with my sister. Snap bang went the screen door.

"Hey, non-existing little tofu-brain," she said. My three fellow cineasts were out in the yard. Viv and Feet were

175

sort of tanning. Harry had a big straw sombrero over his face. I was on my way from the downstairs bathroom to the yard. Ronnie was at the kitchen table, a soup spoon in her left hand, digging up about four peoples' worth of Tin Roof ice cream from a salad bowl.

A siren went by about a block away. I couldn't tell whether it was a fire truck or a police car.

"What is it, my delicate stalk of wheat?" I replied.

Ronnie is a tad oversize, or as my father once said, a bit short for her weight.

"A friend of mine saw the back of your head on TV. She said your ears stuck out so far she thought she was watching a Mickey Mouse Club re-run."

"Being a friend of yours, she gathered her wits and figured out her mistake only two hours after the program was over," I suggested.

"Ho ho. Oh, you are funny. How long are your stupid friends going to be hanging around our place?"

"They have the bad luck to be right-handed, Ronnie," I said. I decided to be serious if she would let me. "They don't want to go home as long as home is the way it is. If home is just a drag, at least you know it's a drag you're used to. But if it's full of ideas from the planet X, you aren't too sure you want to be there."

"Ghmmft yfghhjl," said Ronnie, speaking her favourite words in Tin Roof.

Before I could get to the kitchen door and out I heard a familiar but not overly-pleasing sound. It was a grinding buzzer noise. The button that activates this buzzer is up in my grandmother's room. If you hear the buzzer it means you are supposed to zang up the stairs, because Grandma might have a fishbone stuck in her throat, or she might want you to mail her latest angry letter to the "Mac" show. She gets angry every time the "Mac" show is about embarrassing things. Television should be for educational purposes, she always says. Her favourite program is about these people who have to guess how much motorboats or washing machines cost.

Ronnie could not hear the buzzer, though it was closer to her than it was to me. People who are putting large quantities of frozen butterfat into their face holes cannot hear certain frequencies of sound waves.

I looked outside where my friends were basking, and then I turned and zanged up the stairs. I did them two at a time. At least I got to do that without being yelled at, for once.

When I entered my grandmother's room, she was sitting in her embroidered armchair and banging on the floor with her cane. That is what she does when no one answers the buzzer within fifteen seconds. When she saw me she banged the floor about four more times. Then she hung her cane over the arm of her chair and looked at me across the tops of her new spangle-rimmed eyeglasses.

"Oh, there you are, Orville."

"Neville, Granny," I said, patiently.

"Don't call me Granny. Name's Grandma,"

"You buzzed, Grandma?"

"And don't be cheeky. I called you up here to ask you some serious questions."

"Fire away," I said, and I sort of half-leaned, half-sat on her bed. It was covered with a quilt I had to admit liking. It must have been sewn together from clothes worn out by my ancestors in the seventeenth century or earlier.

"I'm worried about you and your friends," she said, looking severe but also cute. I like severe grandmothers better than severe mothers or sisters.

"I'm not worried about me so much," I said, "but I am a little worried about my friends."

"Don't interrupt," said Grandma. "Now, I've heard you and your friends coming into this house in the wee hours of the middle of the night. I don't like to think about where you have been and what you have been doing. I am afraid you have been hanging around in cafes, drinking coffee."

"As a matter of fact—"

"Or tying cans to the tails of cats. I know what you young people get up to. Putting stones in your snowballs."

"It's July, Grandma," I said.

I think that most of the things that Grandma is worried about kids doing are things that no kids have done since *her* grandparents' day. She's always promising me that I can ride in the rumble seat of our car.

"So what are all those extra children doing in our house?" she enquired, leaning forward in her chair. She thought she was whispering, but you could hear

Grandma's whispers two rooms away. "We seem to have a problem with extra children."

"Actually they have a problem with extra parents," I said, smiling.

"Don't be cheeky," she said.

"Grandma, why did you call me up here?"

"I forget," she said.

Down the stairs I went, two at a time. That's not as enjoyable, but it's better than nothing, better than one at a time.

My father was standing in front of the refrigerator, holding the door open, wondering what he wanted, just the way I was always catching heck for doing. That happens a lot around our place. My mother runs the hot water when she's washing her hands and face, instead of using the plug. She also pulls electric plugs out of the wall by yanking on the cord instead of the plug. My father leaves magazines opened in the middle and bent back.

He pointed at the newspaper on the table. He meant the headline. It said UNUSUAL ENDING TO TELEVISION PROGRAM. I had to agree with him.

"You could have done better than that in your sleep," I said.

"I think I have, on occasion," he said.

He closed the refrigerator door without getting anything out of it. I opened it again and seized a large carton of skim milk. I put the spout to my mouth and glugged down a few swallows.

"I think you have been told about doing that more than a few times," my father said.

"Yeah, but I've seen you doing it," I said.

"That's different. I'm the dad," he said, smiling.

I heard a siren going by about three blocks away. I thought it was a police car for sure.

"What do you think is going to happen?" I asked.

"All good things come to an end," he said.

That was not an unusual answer to come from him. It's one of the reasons I get impatient with him, and also one of the reasons I kind of like him.

"Which reminds me," I said. "I think I'll quit playing the tuba."

"Don't do that." He leaned up close. "It's one of my favourite sounds around here. When you hit C-sharp above the lines it sounds like old Engine Number 444."

"Really?"

"Also, it discourages certain other noises around here."

I put the milk back in the refrigerator and headed for the back yard. I saw my father open the refrigerator door again.

There was my mother coming up the steps to the back porch. She had a shopping bag from the drug store. It contained mainly a couple of cartons of cigarettes. The drug store is the place you go to to get the medicine your doctor prescribes for your rasping cough and chest pains. On your way out you can stop at the cash register and pick up a couple of cartons of cigarettes. Each carton of cigarettes costs about as much as a decent pair of blue jeans and a shirt.

"I didn't do it," I said.

"Do what?" she asked.

She was a little out of breath. She got past me and put her plastic sack on the kitchen table. My father had disappeared.

"Whatever it was, I didn't do it," I said. "I guess you could say I am trying to get a little ahead. I would like to offer a blanket denial, and then whatever comes up, whatever bad thing's been done around here, you can apply my denial to it. I don't even have to be around."

"Look, if you've done something, I would like to know right now," she said. "I'm tired. I've been shopping. I want to sit down and relax."

She meant sit down and have a cigarette.

"Really, Mom, I didn't do anything. Nothing I know of anyway. Well, I drank straight from the milk carton, but Dad already gave me heck for that. It was just a joke."

"Drinking milk from the carton is a joke? I don't get it."

"No, wait. Oh, never mind. I think we kids are going to go to Kannegeiser Beach. We're thinking of camping out here in the yard, if you don't mind, tonight."

A siren was coming closer and closer. It got really loud. It was a police car, right on Bicuspid Avenue. The blue and white car sped by, siren really loud, red and blue lights spinning. Then it lowered in pitch and got quieter and disappeared, in the direction of the park.

"I'm not sure we want a dozen teenagers sprawled all over the lawn every night," said my mother, ripping open a carton of Lucky Cat Super Light cigarettes.

"I'll dozen teenagers you," I said.

"What? What dozen?"

"Just kidding, Mom," I said, and hastened down the steps to the lawn.

We decided that camping out was going to be a last resort, or that my yard would be a resort holiday in case of need, or that we would meet there and re-sort our priorities. We had assorted reasons for going there.

But first we decided to make a round of the parents. Was it because we were brave and wanted to provoke a climax to this interstellar adventure? Was it because we felt that people, especially young people, had to set an example by taking matters into their own hands instead of waiting for the authorities, also known as grownups, to settle matters? Was it because we still kind of suspected that we were characters in a movie, and had the sense to know that movies always end with personal confrontations?

I don't think so. I think we did it for two reasons. One: kids usually wind up going home for some reason. Two:

we were really curious about how this was going to turn out.

First we went to Harry's apartment. You'll remember that Harry just had one extra set of parents. We met one of his mothers on the sidewalk in front of the apartment building. She was wearing Reeboks, a headband, and a Lycra running outfit, every colour under the sun, not to mention neon. She was sweating on the sides of her head. Kind of pretty for a parent.

"Harold," she puffed. "Take off that silly hat."

Harry was wearing a paper party favour hat, blue with a green stripe. He took it off and folded it five times and popped it into his mouth. Then he took a salt shaker from Flics out of his pants pocket, and tilting his head back, shook salt into his open mouth.

We looked on proudly, I guess you might say. Well, why not? We had put up with him this long, and no one forced us to hang around with him.

"You'll choke to death," said Harry's possible mother.

Harry grabbed his own throat in both hands and started throttling himself, his feet kicking out wildly, his eyes bulging. Weird squeaks escaped his mouth. He fell to the ground and lay still, his fingers around his neck.

"Get up from there," said the likely Mrs Fieldstone. "You'll get your clothes and yourself filthy."

Harry took off one of his Nikes and stood up. He put the shoe on his head. He crossed his eyes and stuck out his tongue. He put his thumb into his nostril. He stood on one foot, the one with only three-quarters of a brown sock on it. He made a sound like an ambulance.

I wanted to hightail it out of there.

Harry's probable mother removed the shoe from Harry's head and whacked his backside with it four times, twice on her forehand and twice on her backhand.

Harry straightened up, as much as he could.

"You're my real mom, all right," he said. "Hi."

She handed him his shoe, which he put on, though he did not do up the lace.

"In case all that activity of yours had more purpose than usual," she said, "I can tell you that our two visitors left this afternoon, shortly after watching television."

Next we traipsed over to Viv's place. I liked going to the Lemieux place because they have an old murky pond in the front yard, with lots of goldfish and frogs in it. Neighborhood cats gather in Viv's front yard.

"Have you thought of what you're going to do?" asked Harry. "Want some tips?"

"I'm going to act natural," said Viv, very quietly.

"When are you going to start?" I asked.

"Ho ho, Neville, ho ho."

She was really nervous.

When we got there the place was so still you could hear a cat purr. First we walked all the way round the house.

"It's quiet," whispered Viv, a lot more whispery than usual.

"Too–" started Harry.

Feet clamped her hand over his mouth.

"I'm going inside," said Viv, a look of bravery and low-grade fear in her eyes. For a moment I had the crazy idea that she could have been a movie star, and the even crazier idea that I would like to give her a hug. Can you imagine?

"We're coming in with you, I said."

"We are?" asked Harry.

Feet persuaded him with an adroit application of thumb pain.

"Let's fan out," I suggested, "and each take a room."

But we stayed in a clump and wound up in the middle of the kitchen. There was a note on the kitchen table.

Dear Vivienne, the people from the other side of the universe told us they were leaving, and we decided to go with them. There's frozen bluefish in the fridge. Mom and Dad.

"Oh my gosh!" said Harry, grabbing the hair on the top of his head.

"Harry, it's just a *joke*," said Viv.

We had to walk several blocks up Fogswept Boulevard, because the people who lived there were not the kind of people who would ride a city bus. I could see that Feet was nervous. She stopped once to take off her sandals and shake dirt out of them, but there wasn't any dirt.

I was going to tell her that she didn't have to do this, but she would only have said yes she did.

And then we were at her big white house with the brass door knocker and all the windows. I think we were all hoping that her extra parents would be gone already. No such luck. Feet got her house key from the very easy hiding place she uses, and in we went.

"I'm home!" shouted Feet, and we waited.

In the amount of time it would take to name all the really bad movies Elvis Presley was in, we were joined by four copies of Mrs Corbishly and one copy of Mr Corbishly. You will remember that one Mr Corbishly had left his skin in the back yard, I mean garden, one Mr Corbishly had deflated on TV, and one Mr Corbishly would be downtown in the financial district, closing a deal with some people from the Pacific Rim.

I could see that Feet was getting more and more nervous. Or something like nervous. She was biting at the back of her right hand.

One of the Mrs Corbishlys swooped down on us, her fancy white lounge pyjamas floating in ivory ripples behind her.

"Well, well, well, here you are, Coriander, and all your friends! To what do we owe our gratitude for this lovely surprise?"

Feet took one step back, and started to nibble at the back of her left hand.

"Surely you can talk to your own mother," said the Mr Corbishly.

"Now, there's the problem," said Harry. Out of politeness he was carrying his beaded African cap in his hand. I don't know where it had been till then.

"How's that?" asked the man.

"Well, it all depends on how you define the word mother," said Harry. "And I'm not sure I should ask you for your definition."

"Well," said the man, "Just look at the love in that mother's eyes," he said.

Harry looked.

"Well, I have to admit–" he started.

"And *that* one," said the man.

Feet stamped her foot, but it didn't make much noise in the thick rug. She raised both hands high in the air. Everyone turned and looked at her. She had tears under her eyes.

"We came here to do weird stuff," she said quietly.

Everyone looked at her a little harder.

"I mean, we came here to do weird stuff and see whether we could make the extra mothers and father go back where they came from."

It seemed as if she had finished all she was going to say, but no one was satisfied with that. We all leaned forward a little more and looked at her harder.

"Well, something has been bothering me all day," said Feet, and she seemed to have got her breath and voice under control, if not her feelings. "I started off with great plans to do weird stuff and get most of you out of my hair and enjoy my summer holiday, but now you are all here, and what I was afraid of seems to be true–"

"What's that, dear?" asked one of the mothers gently.

"It's just–I'm afraid–well, all it is is that–oh, I mean, well, I love you," said Feet.

There was an enormous noise all over the ground floor of the house. Air whooshed in every direction, and artificial human skins swooped back and forth, knocking over lamps and wiping pictures off the walls. We kids dropped to the floor, and tried to get under whatever furniture was handy. The noise and damage went on for fifteen seconds, probably, but it seemed like ten times that long. After the last bits of glass had collected at the bottom of a wall, I opened my eyes and saw Viv lying on her stomach with her legs sticking out from under the grand piano. There was the skin of a Mrs Corbishly lying across her calves.

The only remaining Mrs Corbishly was standing in the doorway to the dining room, surveying the rubble and looking annoyed. I tried to imagine my mother looking only annoyed in such a situation.

An hour later we were in the middle of Kaiser Park, on the way to the beach, and we were surrounded by sirens. Police cars and ambulances and fire trucks, all with sirens screaming and honking and blaring and growling, were zanging away in every direction.

We were seeing the power of television. You could have

twenty-meter green monsters from Betelgeuse standing at every bus stop for a week, and there might be a little stir in the newspapers and at city hall council meetings. But put a friendly ideomorph from across the galaxies on television and before you know it there will be sirens all over town.

We didn't know exactly what was going to happen, but I think all four of us had our hunches. And now we were in a strange position, I mean as far as emotions go, you know? When my friends first got extra parents on top of the parents they were already having trouble with, they were far from happy about it. But now we knew everyone's extra parents were deflating all over town. From where we stood we could see three fully-clothed human balloons hanging in the tall maple trees.

I mean we should have been glad to get our parents down to one set per person, but none of us looked happy at all. It was really hard on us to know that these people from a planet without kids were being rejected by the kids and the grownups of this planet. Of this city, anyway.

Because this is what was happening, all over town. People were standing on their heads, walking sideways, eating dirt, wearing their clothes backward, walking around with carrots in their ears, and so on. On Bristle Street eight college boys carried a small Japanese car past a crowd watching a juggler, and four people deflated overhead.

A bunch of businessmen went swimming in their dark blue three-piece suits on the North Shore. When they were finished there were deflated ideocorpses floating in the inlet.

A street singer outside Birkleschneiber's Department Store spent the afternoon eating his guitar, and passers-by littered Rain Street with clothing.

All over town there were people enjoying themselves, inventing new ways to make escaping balloons out of their visitors.

We four young cinema critics decided we would not go to Kannegeiser Beach after all. Instead, we made our way to the university and visited Professor Purzelbaum's office. At first we thought he wasn't there, but then his sugarloaf head appeared from behind a pile of looseleaf binders. He was sitting on the windowsill.

"I've been marking assignments," he said. "I had some pretty good students two years ago."

"You're marking assignments from two years ago?" asked Viv, half-way to the top of her voice. Harry leaned away from her.

"I like to give them a taste of the real world," he said. "When you are studying a celestial body that has been around since the Big Boing, you shouldn't be surprised if a learned journal takes two or three years in telling you whether they are going to publish your article."

"Big Bang," said Feet.

Professor Purzelbaum stood up.

"I stand corrected," he said.

His glasses fell off, and I caught them in a smooth motion that I hoped was appreciated by all my colleagues.

"We've come to talk about the latest situation," said Viv.

"What about it?" asked Professor Purzelbaum.

"Well, I don't know—"

Professor Purzelbaum put down his red pencil and the ring binder. He actually put his arm around Viv's shoulders. I never would have done that.

"There are probably a million planets in this corner of the universe," he said quietly and slowly. "I would bet that there are children on at least a hundred of them."

"Yes, but—" said Harry.

"And that on at least one of them there will be a big supply of children and a small supply of parents. This happens once in a while right here on Earth, after a war, for instance."

I had to ask.

"Professor, when the astronauts looked back at our planet they saw a big blue marble, they said. They said it was nearly all water with a little bit of land here and there."

"So I hear," he said.

"So how come we call it Earth? Why don't we call it Water?"

"Some of us do," he said, mysteriously.

That was how we left things with our learned friend in the lab coat. I hope he was right about the planet with too many kids and not enough parents. I expect that he probably was.

Then I thought he wouldn't make a bad visiting parent himself.

29.

My father went back to work early. He wasn't made for vacations. His first headline went like this: MOTHER SHIP POPS OFF.

My grandmother never found out about the parents from space. She knew something unusual was going on because there were more kids than normal around our house. She told me she was on to us. She said she knew we were throwing firecrackers under the milkman's horse.

My mother burnt a cigarette hole in the livingroom rug. She didn't have time for intergalactic problems.

In the Blam Cafe on Kaiser Street they had a special sandwich called "The Creature from Space." It was basically a BLT with avocado and raisin sauce. Harry had one every day for a week.

In the *Moon* Andrew Marx did a special retrospective review of ten classic space invasion movies. He liked *The Attack of the Potato Monster* above all others.

30.

We were at Flics, the four of us, empty glasses on our table. Viv was staring very hard at a couple of old women who were smoking endless cigarettes, putting them down in their ashtray from time to time while they wiped another layer of red lipstick onto their lips. Viv cleared her throat about as loud as a bull terrier growling at a burglar, but it was all in vain. Viv tried coughing a little, then breaking into a four-star coughing fit. It sounded as if her lungs would fall out on the table in front of her, like the envelopes of two small space parents deflating. Still to no avail. The old women ordered more tea and lit more cigarettes and patted powder on the powder on their cheeks and foreheads.

Harry was reading the end of his movie review. He was wearing a blue knitted tuque with a big orange wool ball on the top of it.

"...Tony Curtis as the young trapeze artist frankly made this reviewer want to regurgitate his Glossette Raisins, but Burt Douglas saved the film with his cool demeanor. It is also rumoured that he performed all his own stunts. While one finds this hard to believe, one must certainly admit that his bare chest, almost always in sight, gives a certain sinewy impression of power. It is rumoured that he is a shoo-in to be at least a finalist when it comes to the Oscar for best performance by a male actor."

Viv turned her regard from the smoke-clouded old women and smiled benignly on Harry.

"That's one of your best reviews yet, Harry. The grammar is very tidy, and I am inclined to want to see that picture when it comes on TV again, probably next week. I'm just a little concerned about the repetition of the word 'rumoured.' Couldn't you use another verb there?"

"That's a verb?" asked Harry.

"Harry, I can't believe that you could write such splendid prose and not know what a verb is," said Viv.

"That's prose?" he asked.

Feet lifted his tuque, slapped him on the top of his head with a copy of *Cahiers du cinema*, and replaced his tuque. She pulled it down over his eyes, and he left it there for a few minutes.

"So, Neville, what movie did you see this week?" asked Viv.

"I didn't see any, except part of *Intestines on Maple Street III* on the Family Channel. My parents were watching it. Well, my father was reading a locomotive magazine from France, but he was in the room while it was on. I didn't see enough of it to write a review. But…"

"But what?"

"I have been kind of fooling around, to see if I can maybe *write* a movie."

"What about?"

"I was thinking of a kind of astronomy-fiction adventure. Sort of like Guido's idea. See, there's these alien pods that float down from space and end up in people's rhubarb patches. After a while a kid steps out and wanders into the house."

"Wow," said Harry, "I can see it."

"You can't see anything," said Viv. "My best friend pulled the wool over your eyes."

Harry yanked his hat off. Then he rolled it up and parked it on the back of his head.

"You see," I went on, as if they had been listening attentively, "pretty soon people are getting crowded out of house and home, because they are getting all these extra kids. I was thinking of calling it *Out of the Cradle, Endlessly Walking.* "

"I like it," said Harry.

"I don't know," said Viv, excitedly.

"People don't have rhubarb patches any more. Not many, anyway," said Feet.

I signalled to Guido to bring another round of raspberry-mint tea, except that Harry asked for a new potato-flavoured mineral water from Mexico.

"Okay, I will think about the rhubarb patches a little more. Maybe I will just have them hibernating under the globe thistle. Or *echinops*, as some of us call it."

Feet shot me a mean look. Then she shot me a kick under the table. I would have settled for the mean look.

"Okay," said Guido, "who's having the potato water?"

Viv looked up at him with her red hair hanging in front of her eyes.

"You've got to be kidding," she said.

About the author

Distinguished two-time winner of the Governor General's Award for both poetry and fiction, prolific author George Bowering resides in his native British Columbia, where he teaches at Simon Fraser University–and continues to write and play ball.